THE SMURFS AND THE HOWLIBIRD

SNAPP
The poor stork!
She's going to get smurfed!
Quick! This is our chance to smurf to the old tower!

A SMURFS GRAPHIC NOVEL BY PEYO AND GOS

PAPERCUTZ™
NEW YORK

SMURFS GRAPHIC NOVELS AVAILABLE FROM PAPERCUTZ ™

1. **THE PURPLE SMURFS**
2. **THE SMURFS AND THE MAGIC FLUTE**
3. **THE SMURF KING**
4. **THE SMURFETTE**
5. **THE SMURFS AND THE EGG**
6. **THE SMURFS AND THE HOWLIBIRD**
7. **THE ASTRO SMURF**

COMING SOON:

8. **THE SMURF APPRENTICE**
9. **GARGAMEL AND THE SMURFS**

The Smurfs graphic novels are available in paperback for $5.99 each and in hardcover for $10.99 each. Available at booksellers everywhere.

Or order from us: please add $4.00 for postage and handling for the first book, add $1.00 for each additional book. Please make check payable to NBM Publishing. Send to: PAPERCUTZ, 40 Exchange Place, Suite 1308 New York, NY 10005 [1-800-886-1223]

WWW.PAPERCUTZ.COM

THE SMURFS AND THE HOWLIBIRD))

SMURF™ © *Peyo* - 2011 - Licensed through Lafig Belgium -

English translation Copyright © 2011 by Papercutz. All rights reserved.

"The Smurfs and the Howlibird"
BY PEYO AND GOS

"The Smurf Express"
BY PEYO

"You Can't Smurf in the Way of Progress"
BY PEYO

Joe Johnson, SMURFLATIONS
Adam Grano, SMURFIC DESIGN
Janice Chiang, LETTERING SMURFETTE
Matt. Murray, SMURF CONSULTANT
Michael Petranek, ASSOCIATE SMURF
Jim Salicrup, SMURF-IN-CHIEF

PAPERBACK EDITION ISBN: 978-1-59707-260-1
HARDCOVER EDITION ISBN: 978-1-59707-261-8

PRINTED IN THE USA JULY 2011 BY LIFETOUCH PRINTING
5126 FOREST HILLS CT., LOVES PARK, IL 61111

DISTRIBUTED BY MACMILLAN
THIRD PAPERCUTZ PRINTING

THE SMURFS AND THE HOWLIBIRD

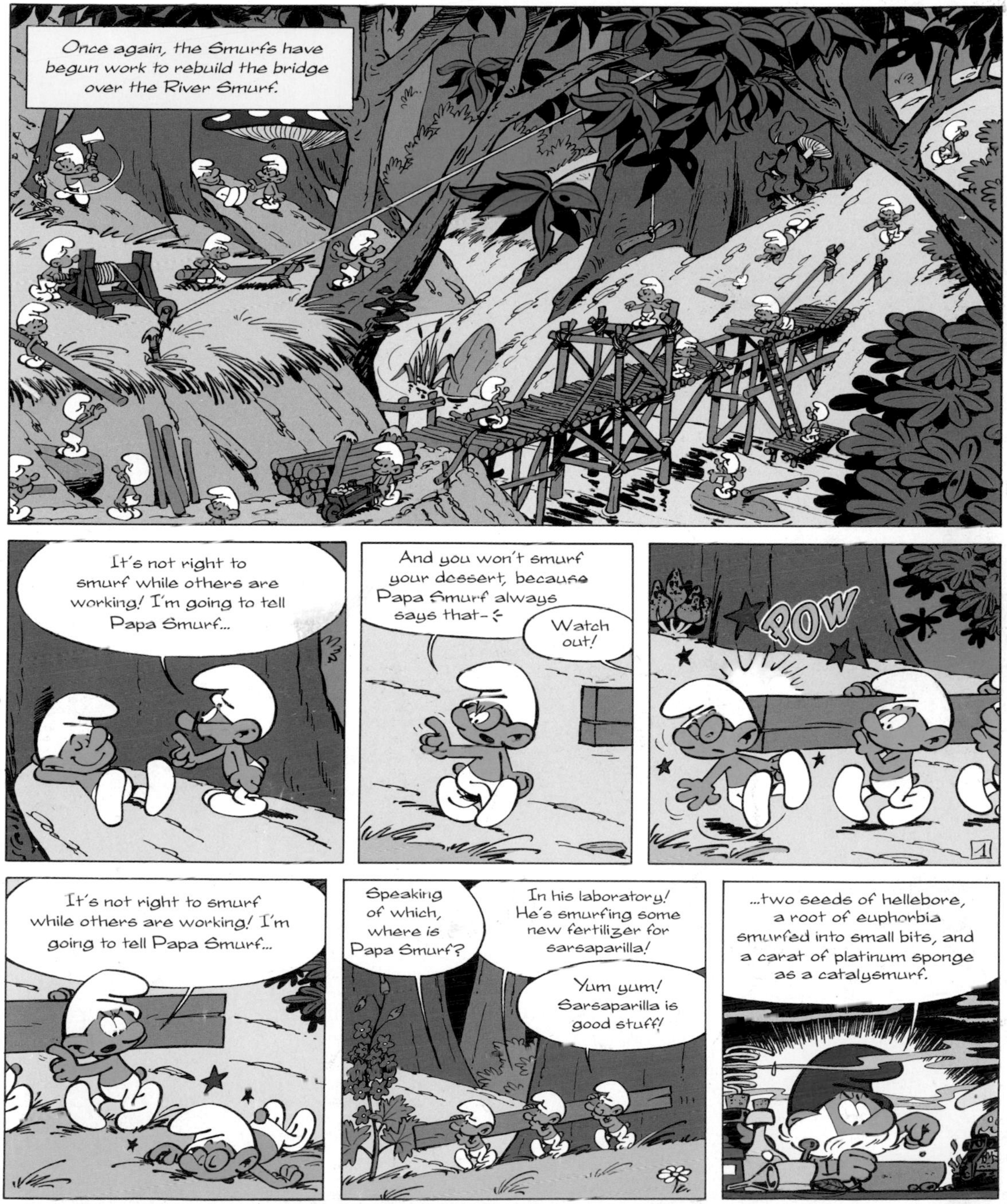

Once again, the Smurfs have begun work to rebuild the bridge over the River Smurf.
It's not right to smurf while others are working! I'm going to tell Papa Smurf...
And you won't smurf your dessert, because Papa Smurf always says that-
Watch out!
POW
1
It's not right to smurf while others are working! I'm going to tell Papa Smurf...
Speaking of which, where is Papa Smurf?
In his laboratory! He's smurfing some new fertilizer for sarsaparilla!
Yum yum! Sarsaparilla is good stuff!
...two seeds of hellebore, a root of euphorbia smurfed into small bits, and a carat of platinum sponge as a catalysmurf.

Strange! What a weird reaction!

SMOOOFF

And voila! Now I just have to smurf the effectiveness of this new fertilizer.

Let's smurf a drop on this daisy!

It doesn't look like... Oh! Yes! It looks like it's getting bigger!

YESSS! I SUCCEEDED!

Eh? What's happening?

Not good...

That transformation isn't normal! Did I smurf a mistake in my formulas?

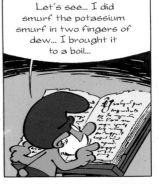

Let's see... I did smurf the potassium smurf in two fingers of dew... I brought it to a boil...

...and I...

?

!

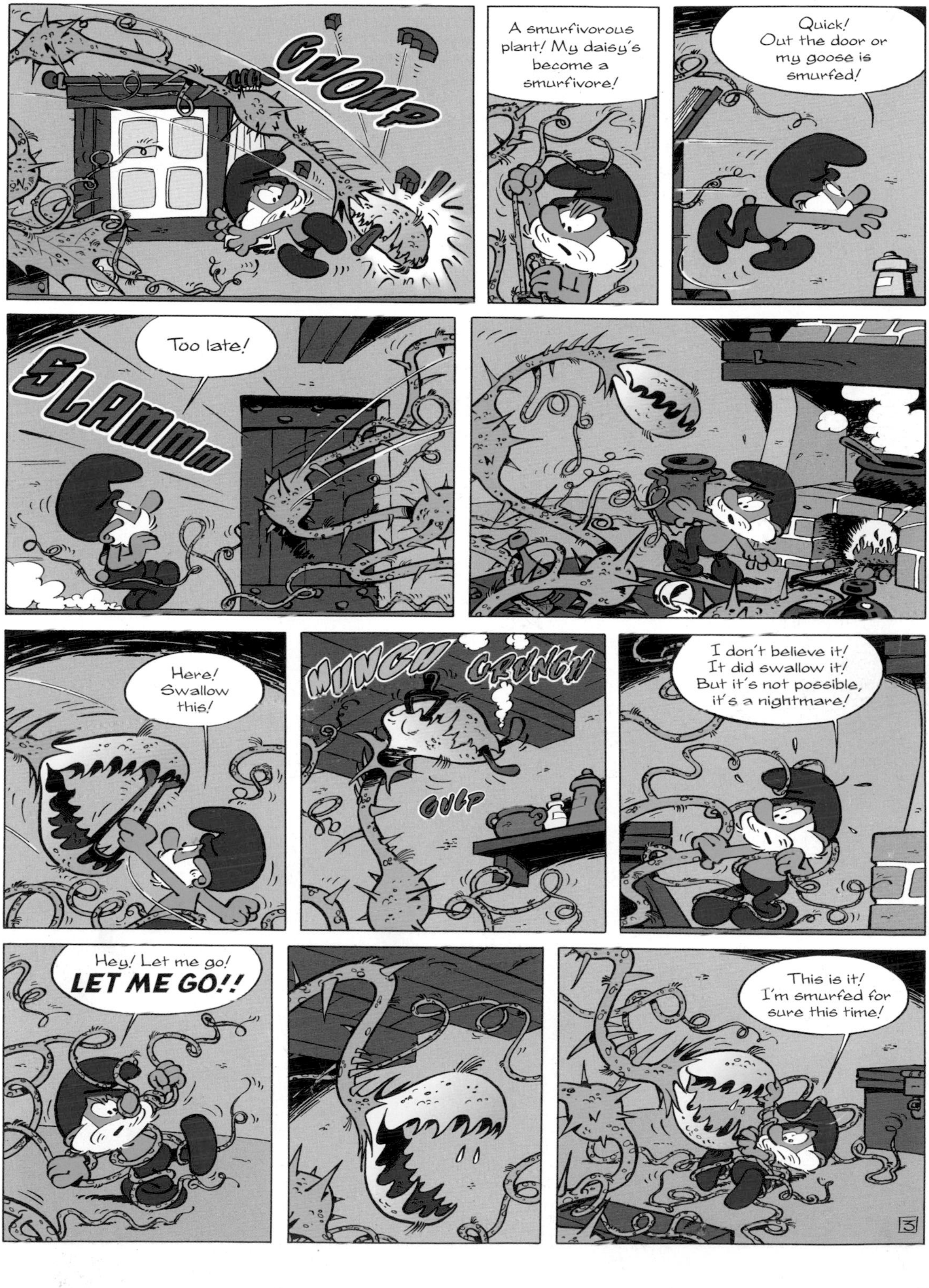

CHOMP
A smurfivorous plant! My daisy's become a smurfivore!
Quick! Out the door or my goose is smurfed!
Too late!
SLAMMM
Here! Swallow this!
MUNCH
CRUNCH
GULP
I don't believe it! It did swallow it! But it's not possible, it's a nightmare!
Hey! Let me go! LET ME GO!!
This is it! I'm smurfed for sure this time!

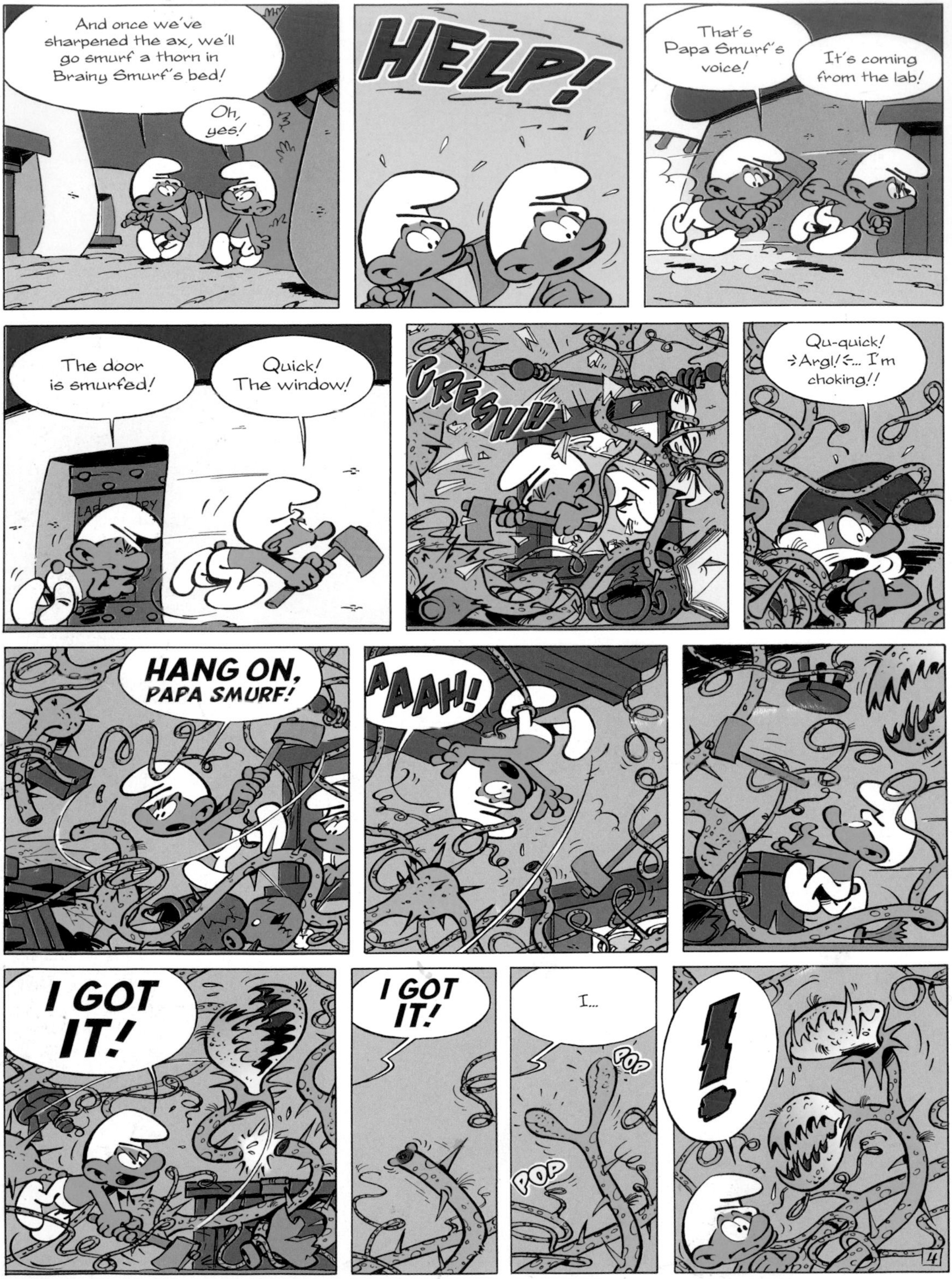
And once we've sharpened the ax, we'll go smurf a thorn in Brainy Smurf's bed!
Oh, yes!
HELP!
That's Papa Smurf's voice!
It's coming from the lab!
The door is smurfed!
Quick! The window!
CRESHH
Qu-quick! Argl! ... I'm choking!!
HANG ON, PAPA SMURF!
AAAH!
I GOT IT!
I GOT IT!
I...
POP
POP
!
4

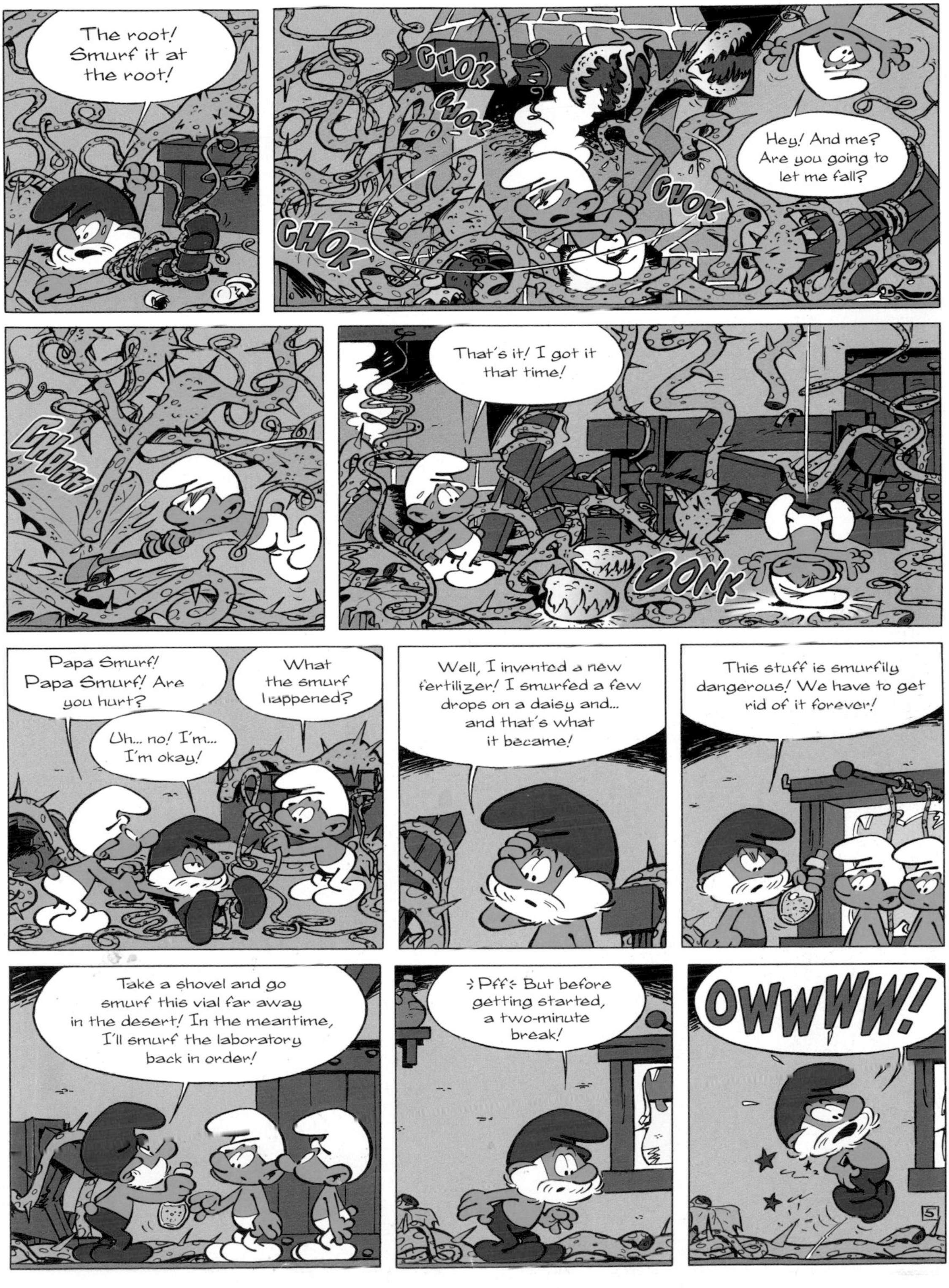
The root! Smurf it at the root!
CHOK
CHOK
CHOK
CHOK
Hey! And me? Are you going to let me fall?
That's it! I got it that time!
BONK
Papa Smurf! Papa Smurf! Are you hurt?
What the smurf happened?
Uh... no! I'm... I'm okay!
Well, I invented a new fertilizer! I smurfed a few drops on a daisy and... and that's what it became!
This stuff is smurfily dangerous! We have to get rid of it forever!
Take a shovel and go smurf this vial far away in the desert! In the meantime, I'll smurf the laboratory back in order!
Pff But before getting started, a two-minute break!
OWWWW!

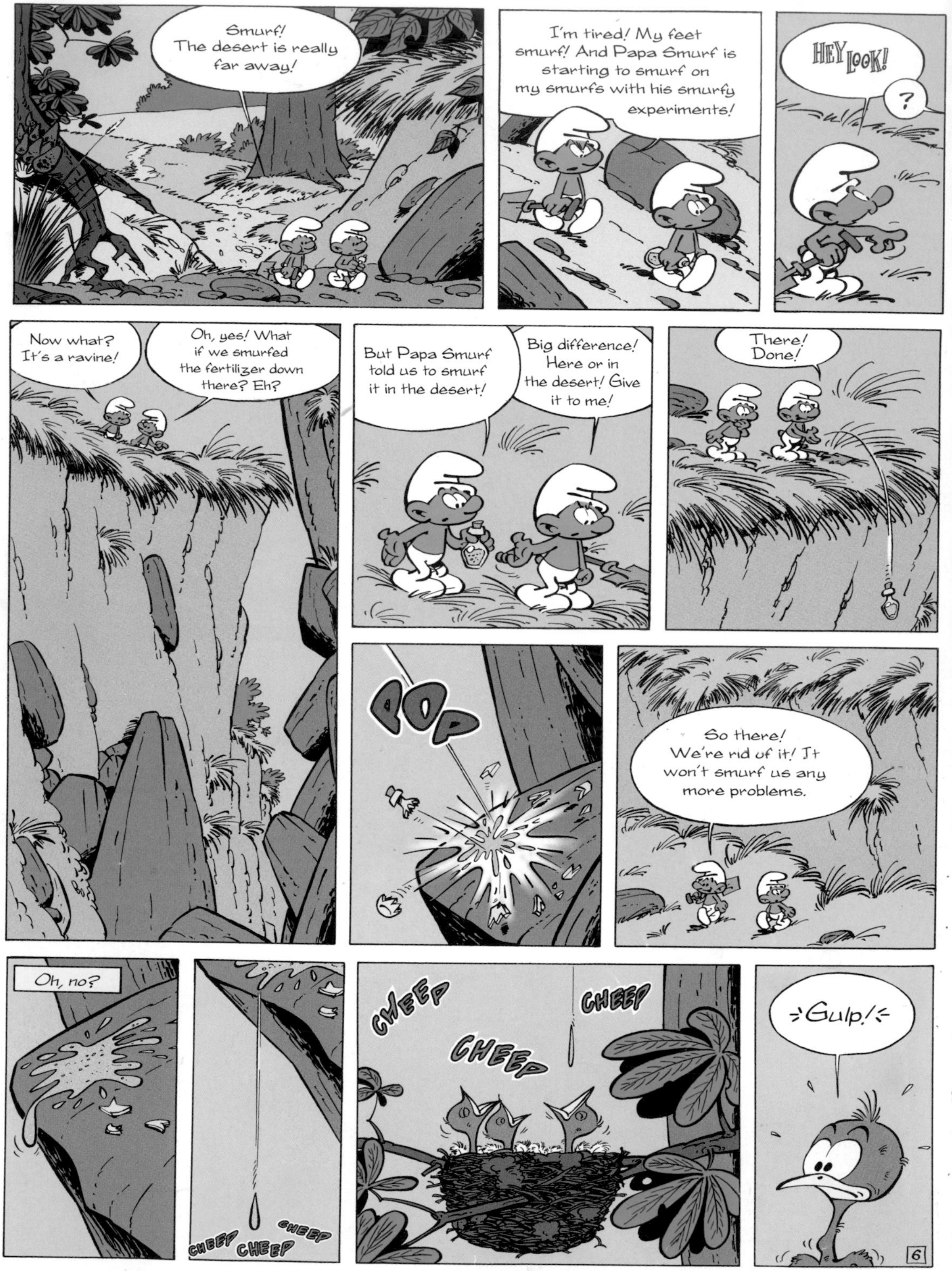
Smurf! The desert is really far away!
I'm tired! My feet smurf! And Papa Smurf is starting to smurf on my smurfs with his smurfy experiments!
HEY LOOK!
?
Now what? It's a ravine!
Oh, yes! What if we smurfed the fertilizer down there? Eh?
But Papa Smurf told us to smurf it in the desert!
Big difference! Here or in the desert! Give it to me!
There! Done!
POP
So there! We're rid of it! It won't smurf us any more problems.
Oh, no?
CHEEP CHEEP CHEEP
CHEEP
CHEEP
CHEEP
Gulp!
6

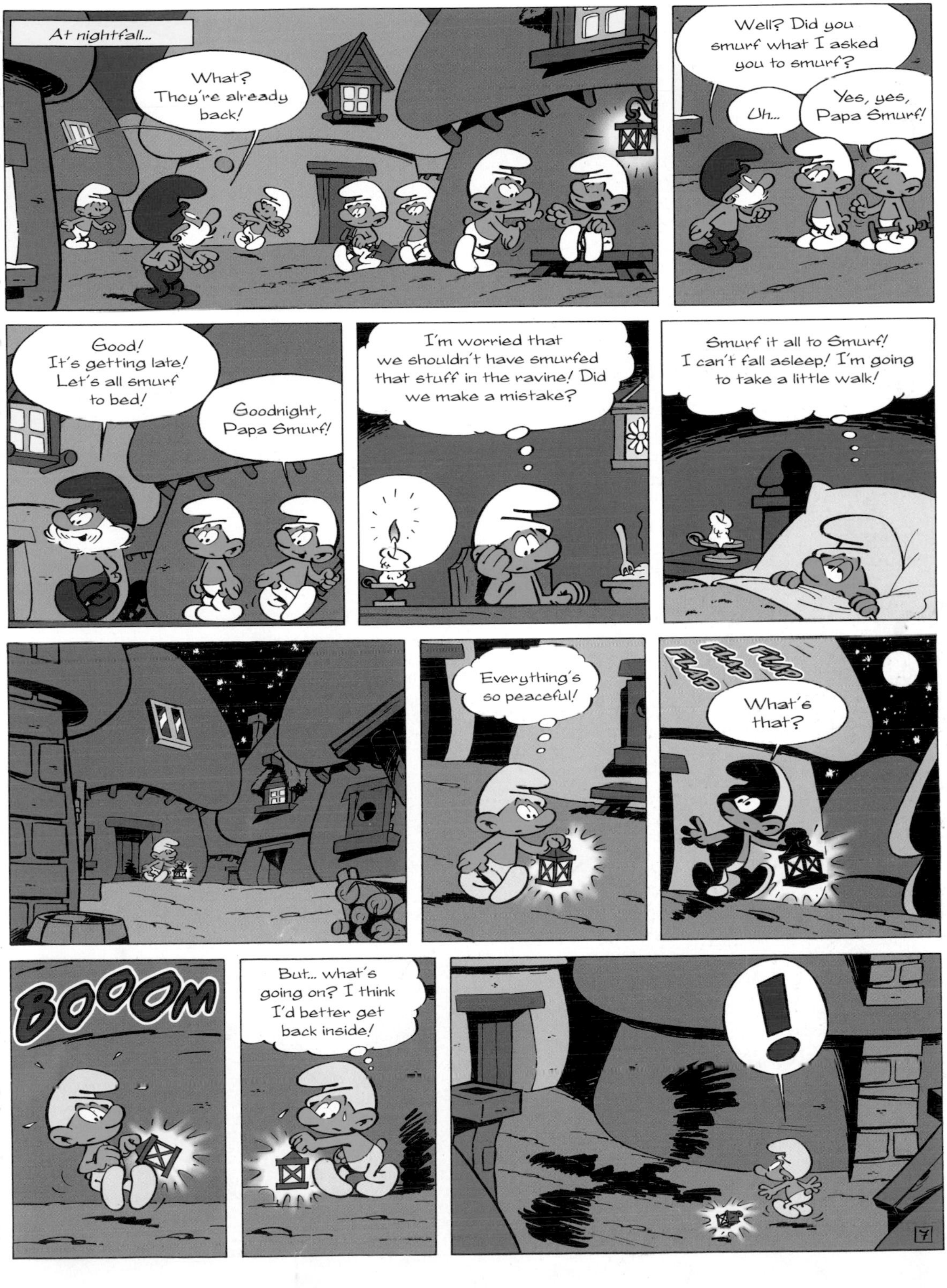

At nightfall...
What? They're already back!
Well? Did you smurf what I asked you to smurf?
Uh...
Yes, yes, Papa Smurf!
Good! It's getting late! Let's all smurf to bed!
Goodnight, Papa Smurf!
I'm worried that we shouldn't have smurfed that stuff in the ravine! Did we make a mistake?
Smurf it all to Smurf! I can't fall asleep! I'm going to take a little walk!
Everything's so peaceful!
FLAP FLAP FLAP
What's that?
BOOOM
But... what's going on? I think I'd better get back inside!
!
7

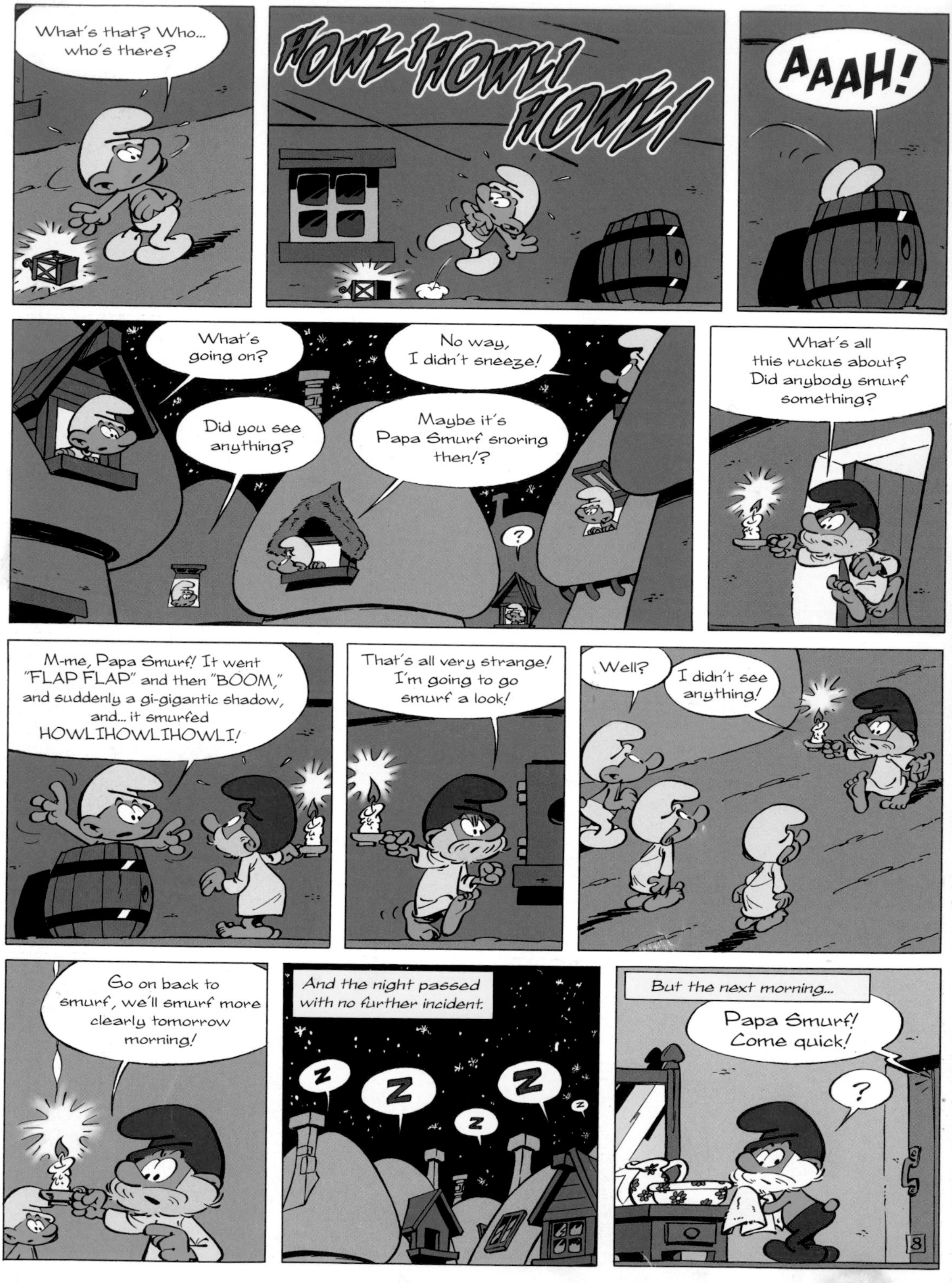
What's that? Who... who's there?
HOWLI HOWLI HOWLI
AAAH!
What's going on?
No way, I didn't sneeze!
Did you see anything?
Maybe it's Papa Smurf snoring then!?
?
What's all this ruckus about? Did anybody smurf something?
M-me, Papa Smurf! It went "FLAP FLAP" and then "BOOM," and suddenly a gi-gigantic shadow, and... it smurfed HOWLIHOWLIHOWLI!
That's all very strange! I'm going to go smurf a look!
Well?
I didn't see anything!
Go on back to smurf, we'll smurf more clearly tomorrow morning!
And the night passed with no further incident.
Z Z Z Z z
But the next morning...
Papa Smurf! Come quick!
?
8

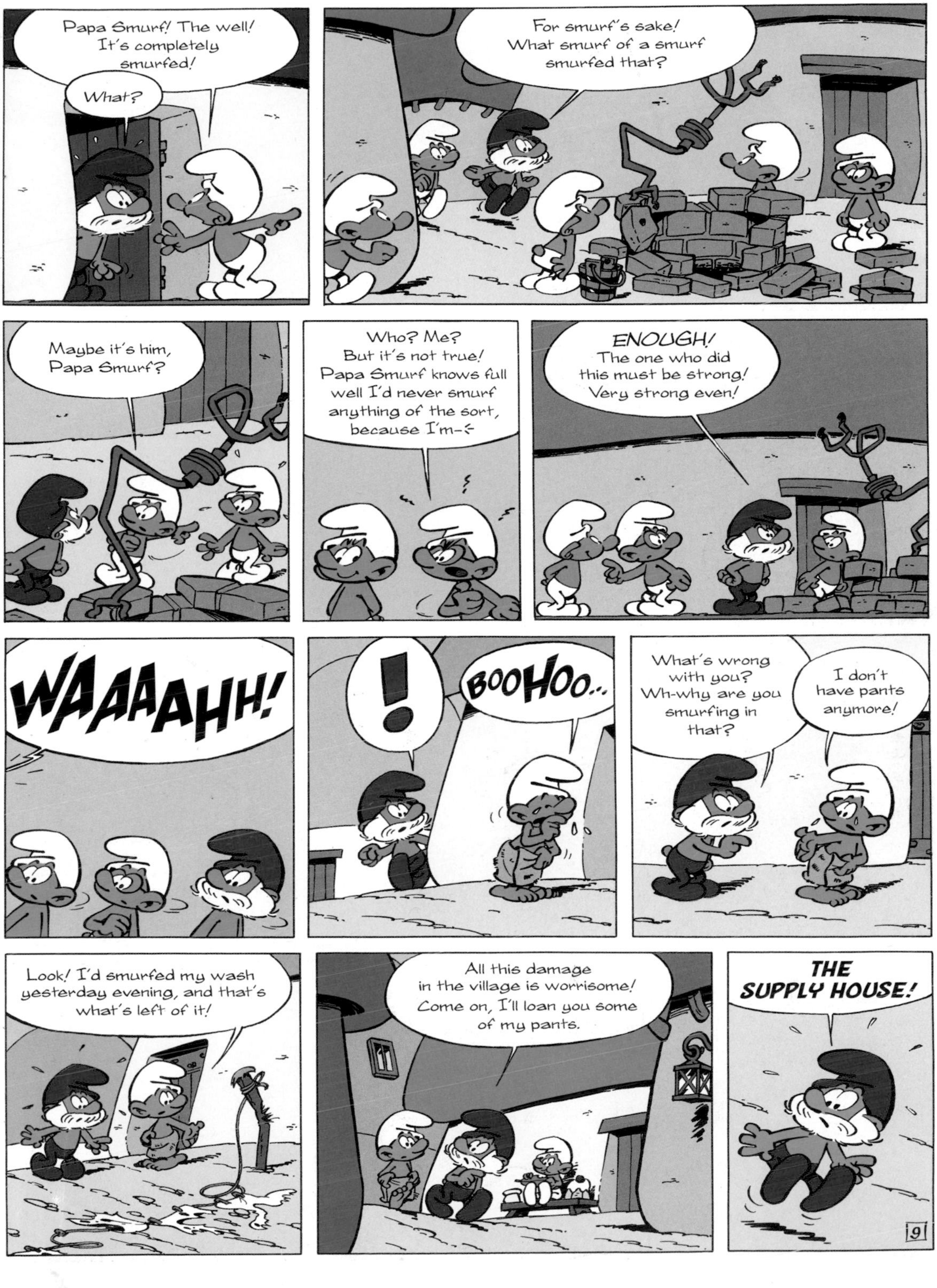
Papa Smurf! The well! It's completely smurfed!
What?
For smurf's sake! What smurf of a smurf smurfed that?
Maybe it's him, Papa Smurf?
Who? Me? But it's not true! Papa Smurf knows full well I'd never smurf anything of the sort, because I'm-
ENOUGH! The one who did this must be strong! Very strong even!
WAAAAHH!
!
BOOHOO...
What's wrong with you? Wh-why are you smurfing in that?
I don't have pants anymore!
Look! I'd smurfed my wash yesterday evening, and that's what's left of it!
All this damage in the village is worrisome! Come on, I'll loan you some of my pants.
THE SUPPLY HOUSE!
9

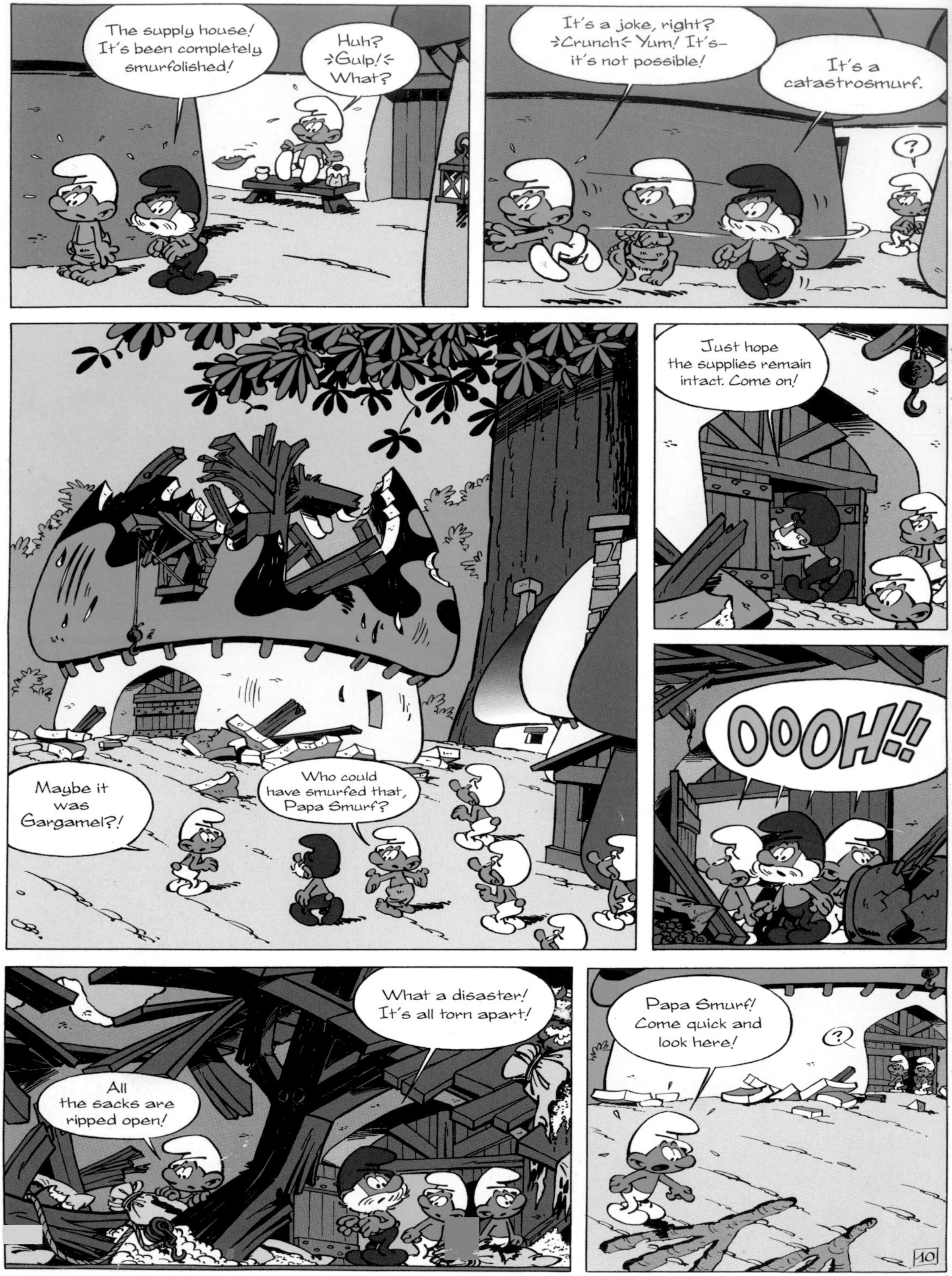
The supply house! It's been completely smurfolished!
Huh? >Gulp!< What?
It's a joke, right? >Crunch< Yum! It's- it's not possible!
It's a catastrosmurf.
?
Just hope the supplies remain intact. Come on!
Maybe it was Gargamel?!
Who could have smurfed that, Papa Smurf?
OOOH!!
What a disaster! It's all torn apart!
All the sacks are ripped open!
Papa Smurf! Come quick and look here!
?
10

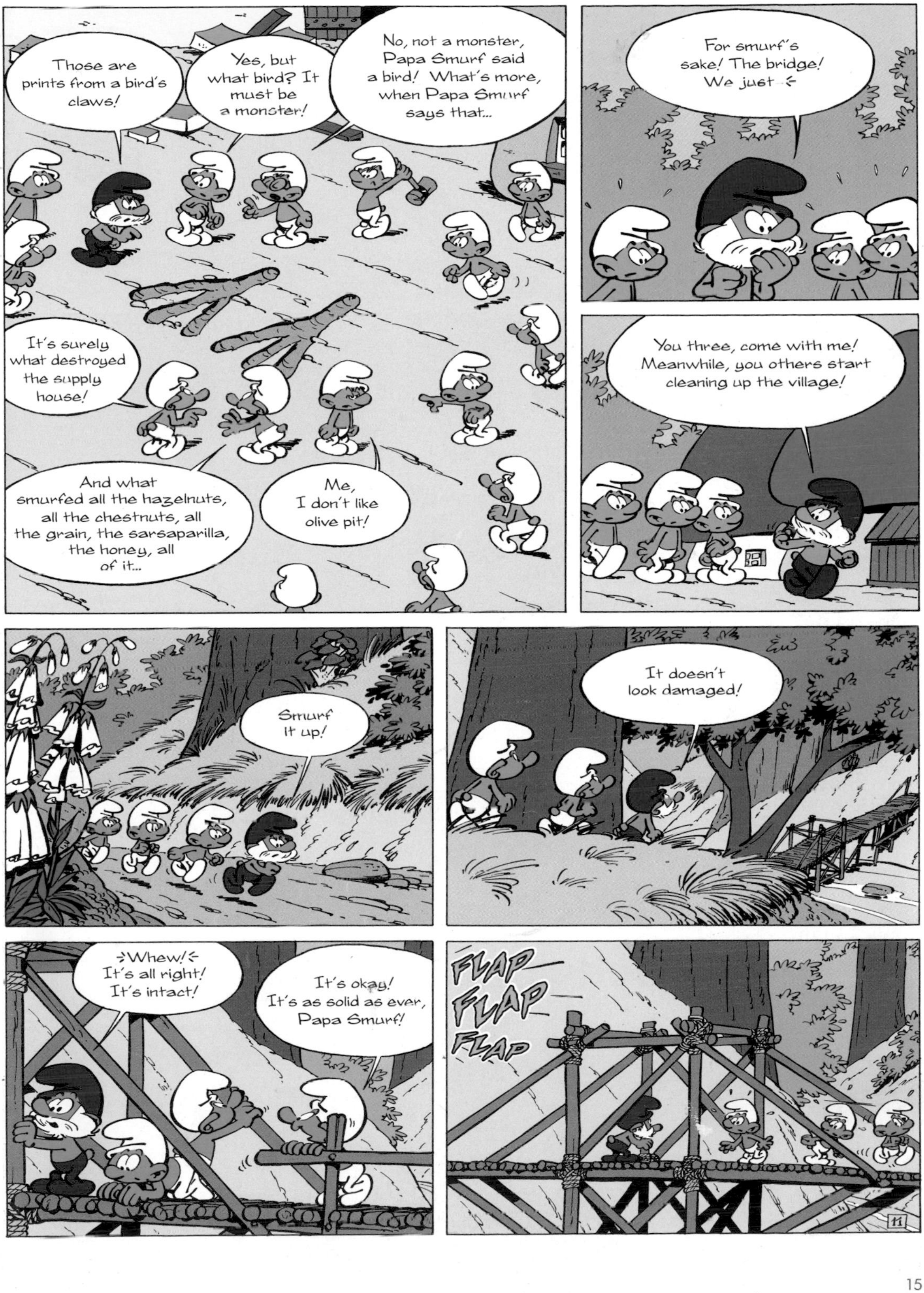

Those are prints from a bird's claws!
Yes, but what bird? It must be a monster!
No, not a monster, Papa Smurf said a bird! What's more, when Papa Smurf says that...
It's surely what destroyed the supply house!
And what smurfed all the hazelnuts, all the chestnuts, all the grain, the sarsaparilla, the honey, all of it...
Me, I don't like olive pit!
For smurf's sake! The bridge! We just...
You three, come with me! Meanwhile, you others start cleaning up the village!
Smurf it up!
It doesn't look damaged!
Whew! It's all right! It's intact!
It's okay! It's as solid as ever, Papa Smurf!
FLAP FLAP FLAP
11

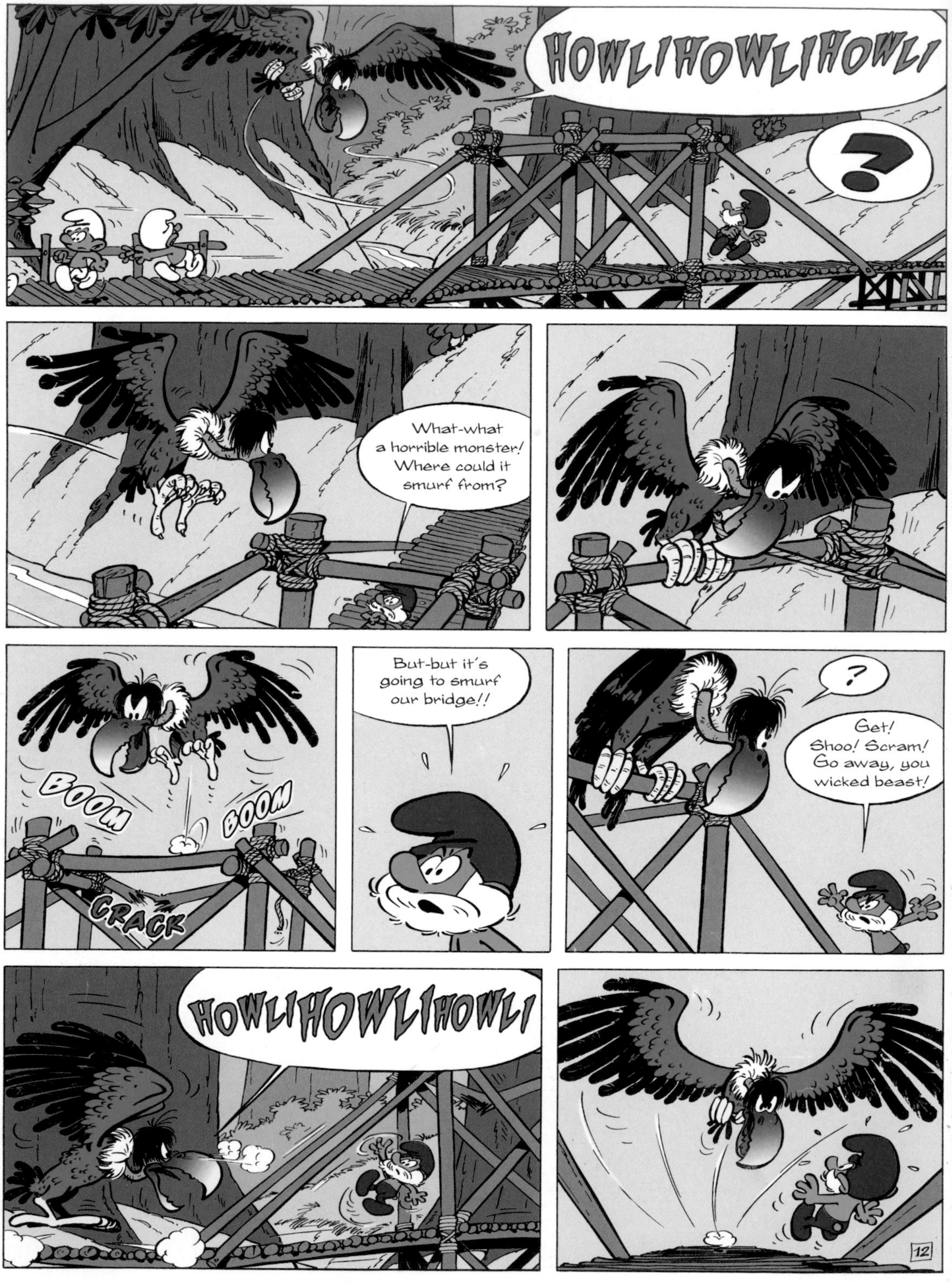
HOWLIHOWLIHOWLI
?
What-what a horrible monster! Where could it smurf from?
BOOM
BOOM
CRACK
But-but it's going to smurf our bridge!!
?
Get! Shoo! Scram! Go away, you wicked beast!
HOWLIHOWLIHOWLI
12

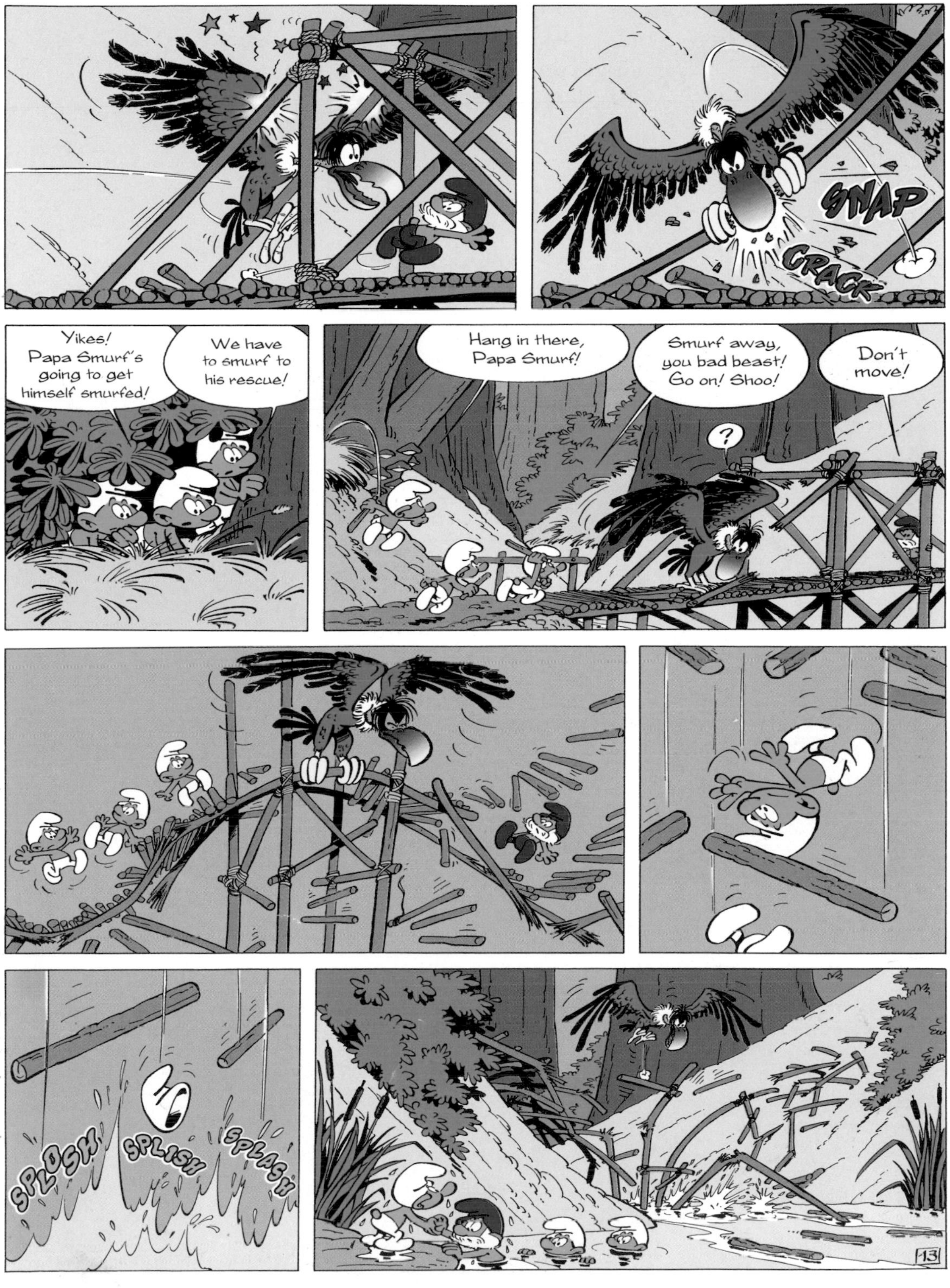
SNAP
CRACK
Yikes! Papa Smurf's going to get himself smurfed!
We have to smurf to his rescue!
Hang in there, Papa Smurf!
Smurf away, you bad beast! Go on! Shoo!
Don't move!
?
SPLOSH
SPLISH
SPLASH
13

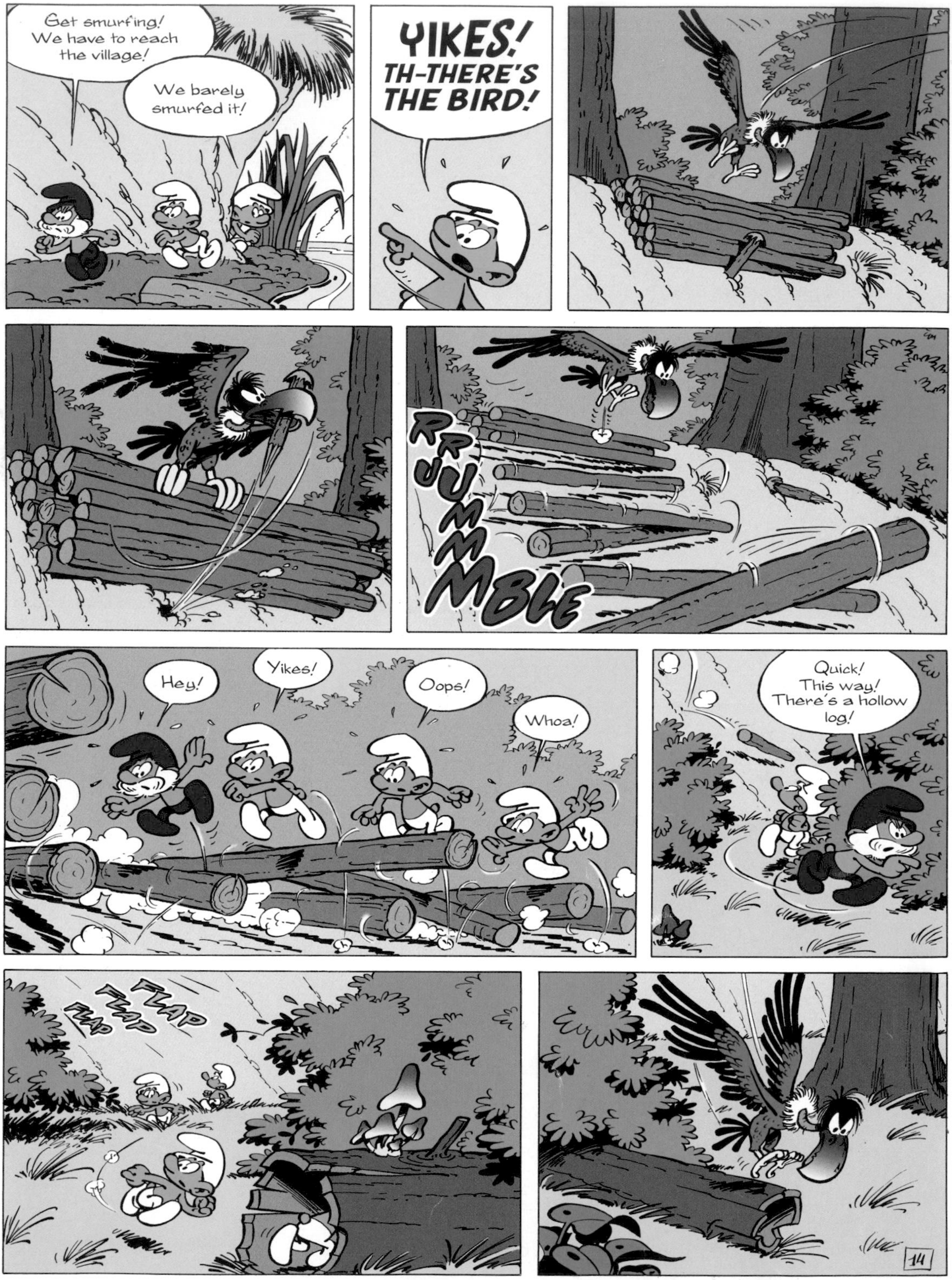
Get smurfing! We have to reach the village!
We barely smurfed it!
YIKES! TH-THERE'S THE BIRD!
RRRUMMMBLE
Hey!
Yikes!
Oops!
Whoa!
Quick! This way! There's a hollow log!
FLAP FLAP FLAP
14

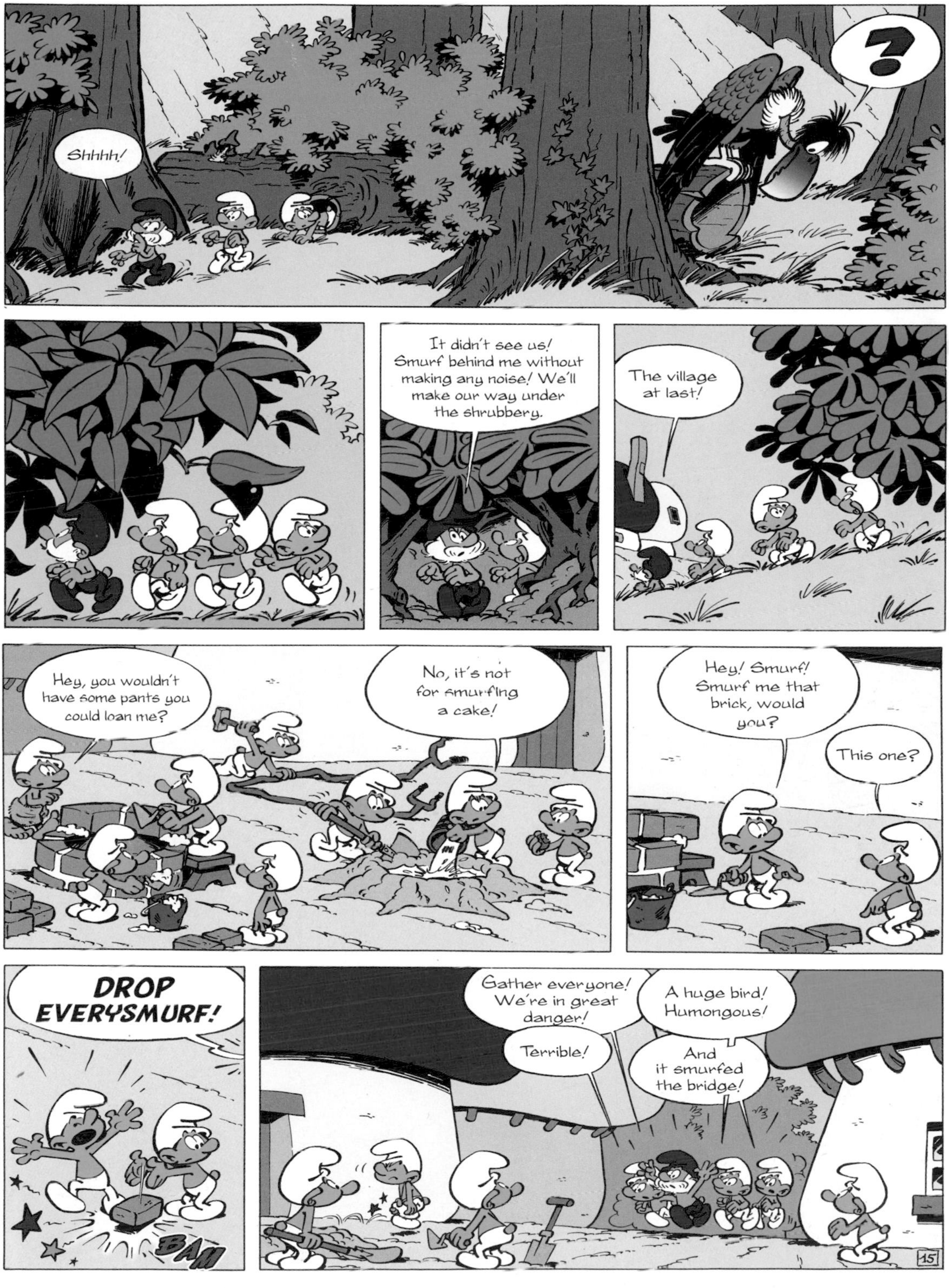
Shhhh!
?
It didn't see us! Smurf behind me without making any noise! We'll make our way under the shrubbery.
The village at last!
Hey, you wouldn't have some pants you could loan me?
No, it's not for smurfing a cake!
Hey! Smurf! Smurf me that brick, would you?
This one?
DROP EVERYSMURF!
BAM
Gather everyone! We're in great danger!
Terrible!
A huge bird! Humongous!
And it smurfed the bridge!
15

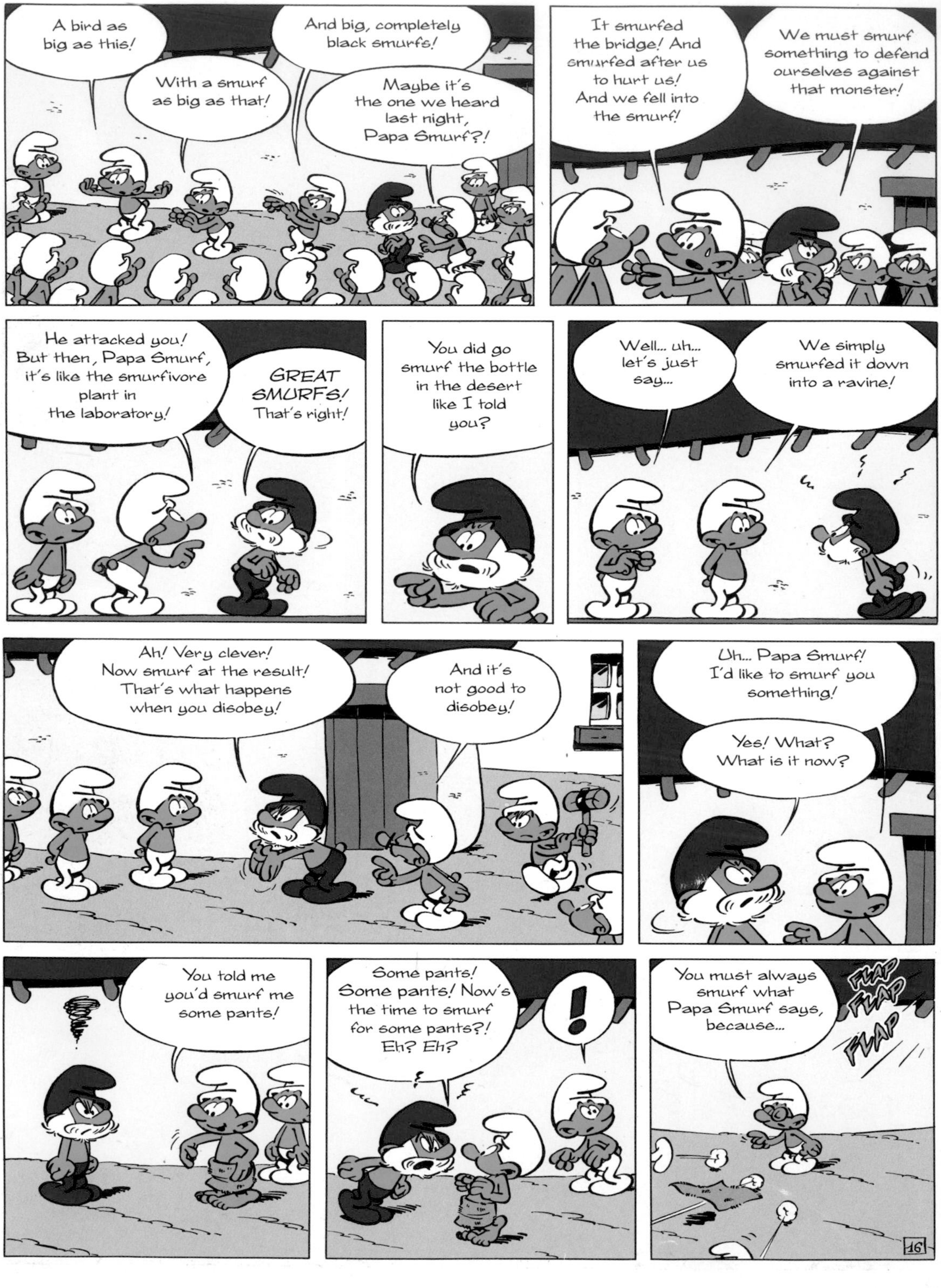
A bird as big as this!
With a smurf as big as that!
And big, completely black smurfs!
Maybe it's the one we heard last night, Papa Smurf?!
It smurfed the bridge! And smurfed after us to hurt us! And we fell into the smurf!
We must smurf something to defend ourselves against that monster!
He attacked you! But then, Papa Smurf, it's like the smurfivore plant in the laboratory!
GREAT SMURFS! That's right!
You did go smurf the bottle in the desert like I told you?
Well... uh... let's just say...
We simply smurfed it down into a ravine!
Ah! Very clever! Now smurf at the result! That's what happens when you disobey!
And it's not good to disobey!
Uh... Papa Smurf! I'd like to smurf you something!
Yes! What? What is it now?
You told me you'd smurf me some pants!
Some pants! Some pants! Now's the time to smurf for some pants?! Eh? Eh?
!
You must always smurf what Papa Smurf says, because...
FLAP FLAP FLAP
16

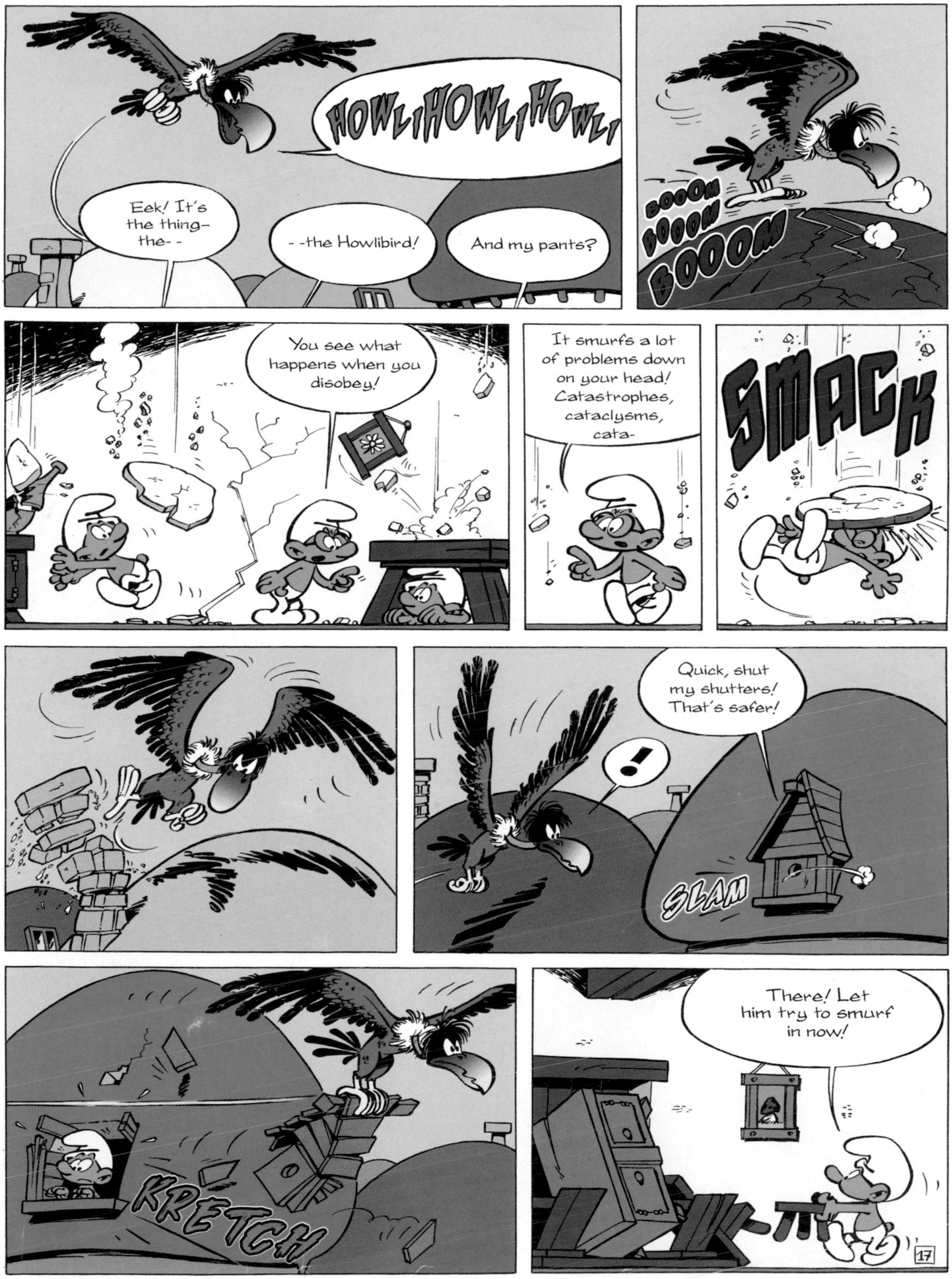
HOWLI HOWLI HOWLI
Eek! It's the thing— the--
--the Howlibird!
And my pants?
BOOOM BOOOM BOOOM
You see what happens when you disobey!
It smurfs a lot of problems down on your head! Catastrophes, cataclysms, cata-
SMACK
Quick, shut my shutters! That's safer!
!
SLAM
KRETCH
There! Let him try to smurf in now!
17

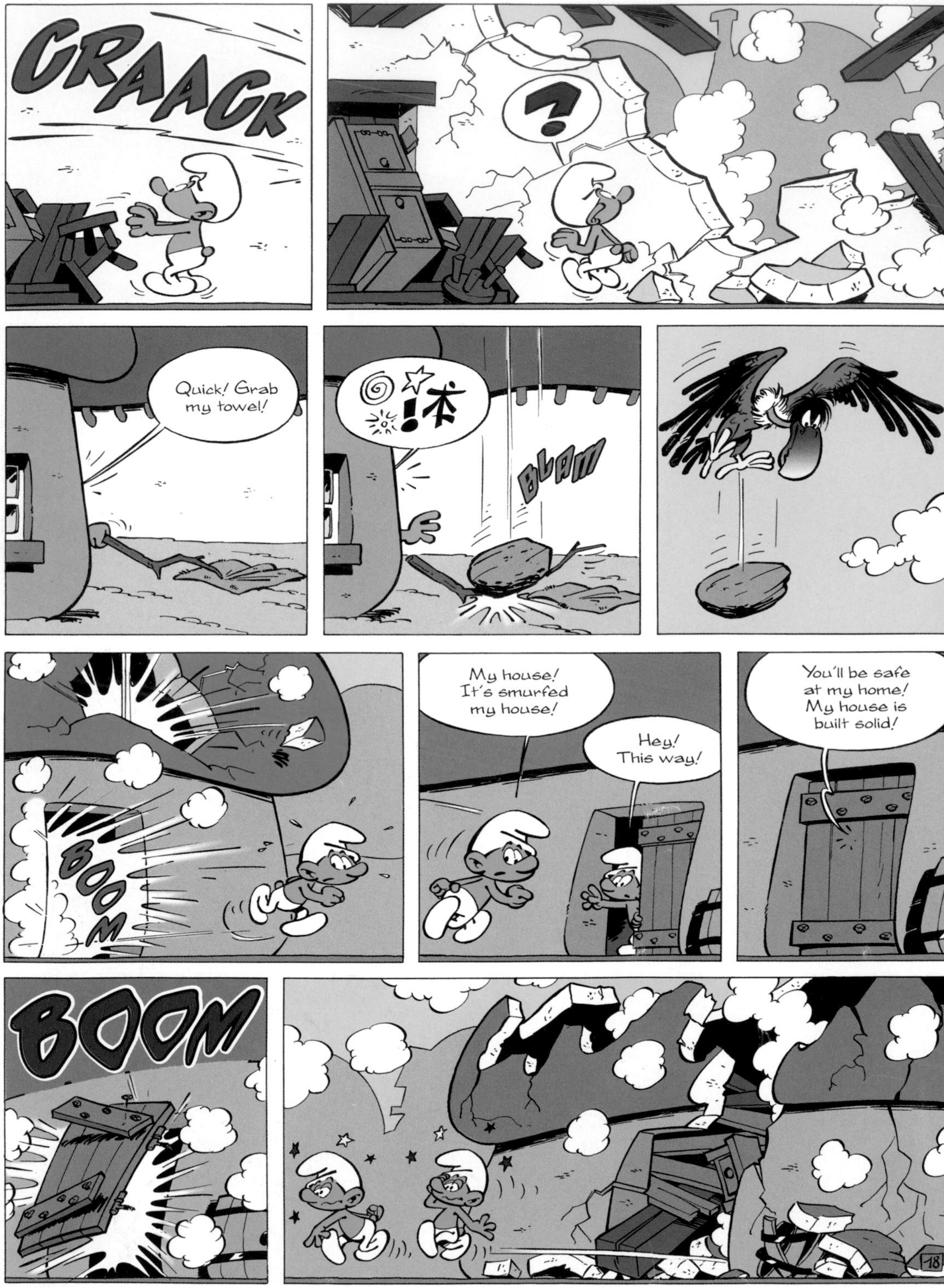
CRAACK
?
Quick! Grab my towel!
BLAM
BOOM
My house! It's smurfed my house!
Hey! This way!
You'll be safe at my home! My house is built solid!
BOOM
18

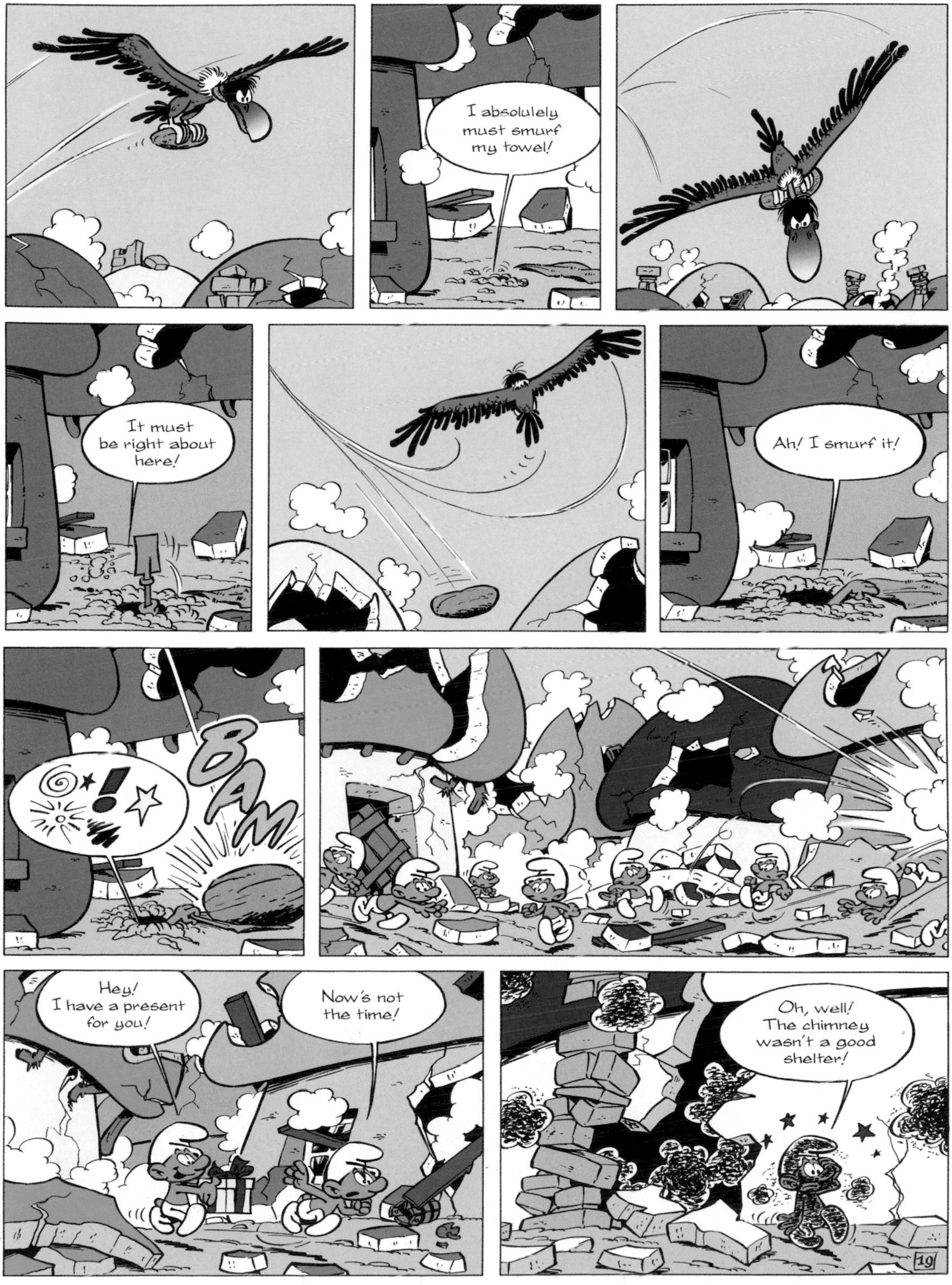
I absolulely must smurf my towel!
It must be right about here!
Ah! I smurf it!
BAM
Hey! I have a present for you!
Now's not the time!
Oh, well! The chimney wasn't a good shelter!
19

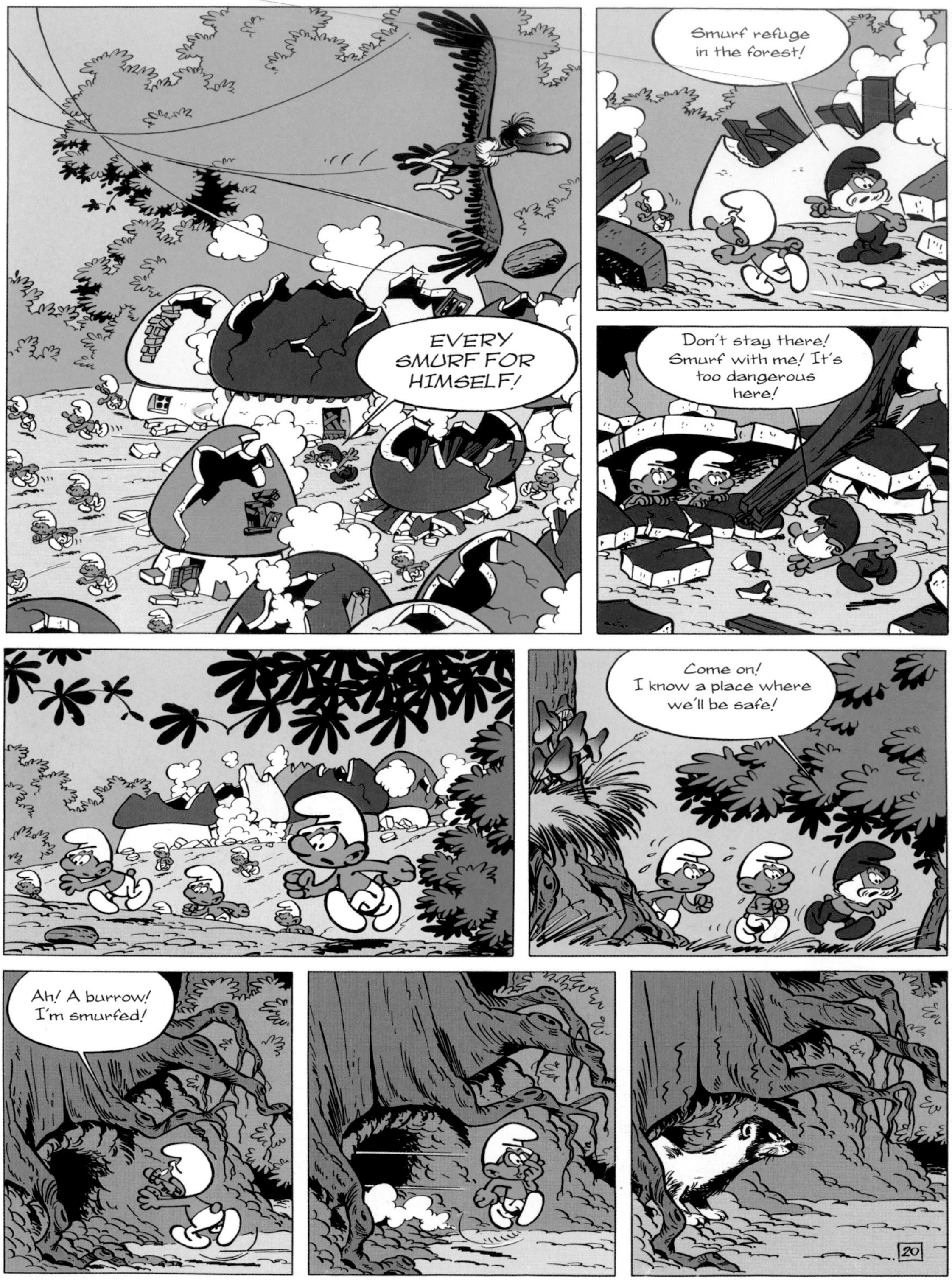
EVERY SMURF FOR HIMSELF!
Smurf refuge in the forest!
Don't stay there! Smurf with me! It's too dangerous here!
Come on! I know a place where we'll be safe!
Ah! A burrow! I'm smurfed!
20

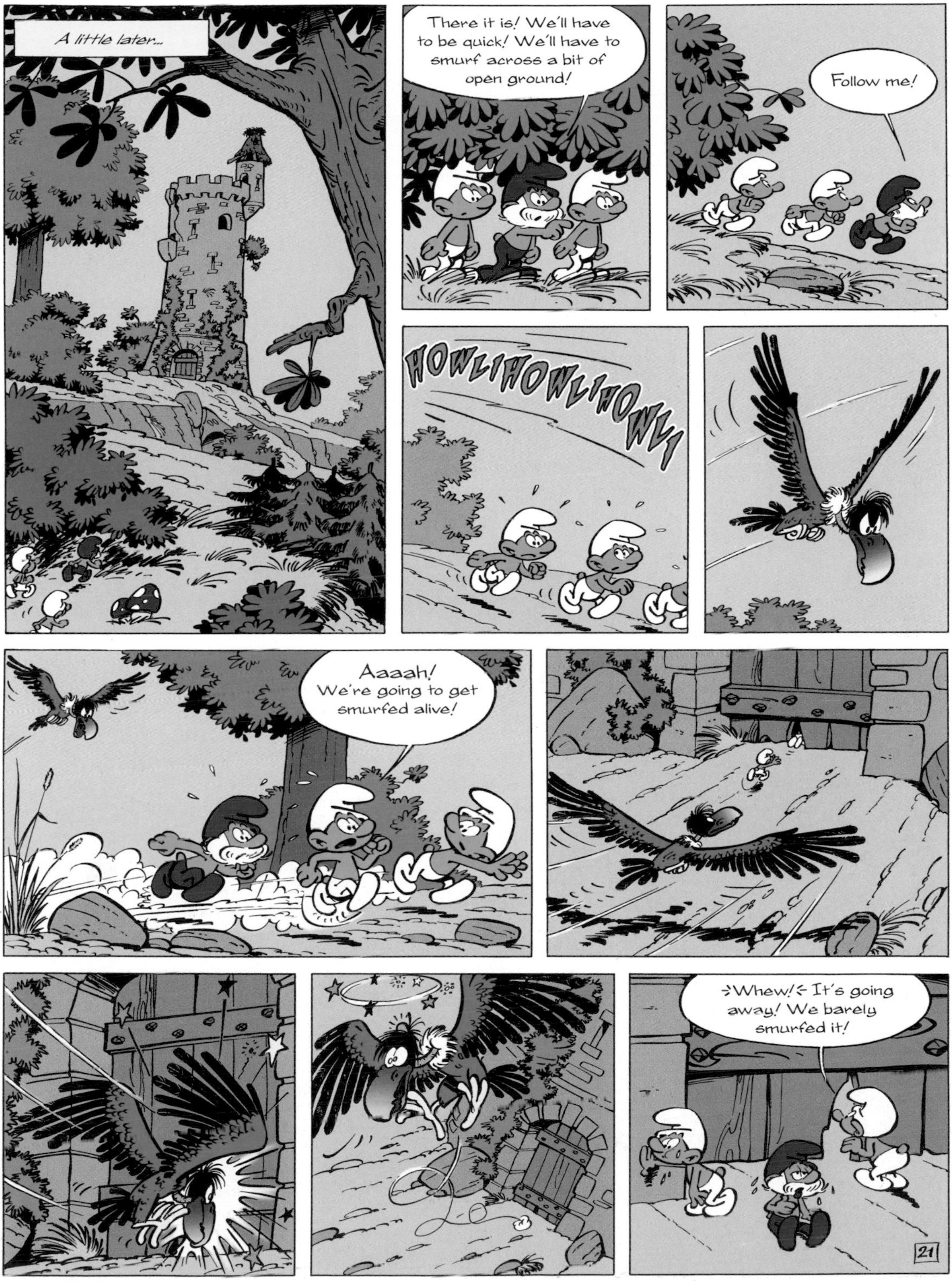
A little later...
There it is! We'll have to be quick! We'll have to smurf across a bit of open ground!
Follow me!
HOWLIHOWLIHOWLI
Aaaah! We're going to get smurfed alive!
Whew! It's going away! We barely smurfed it!
21

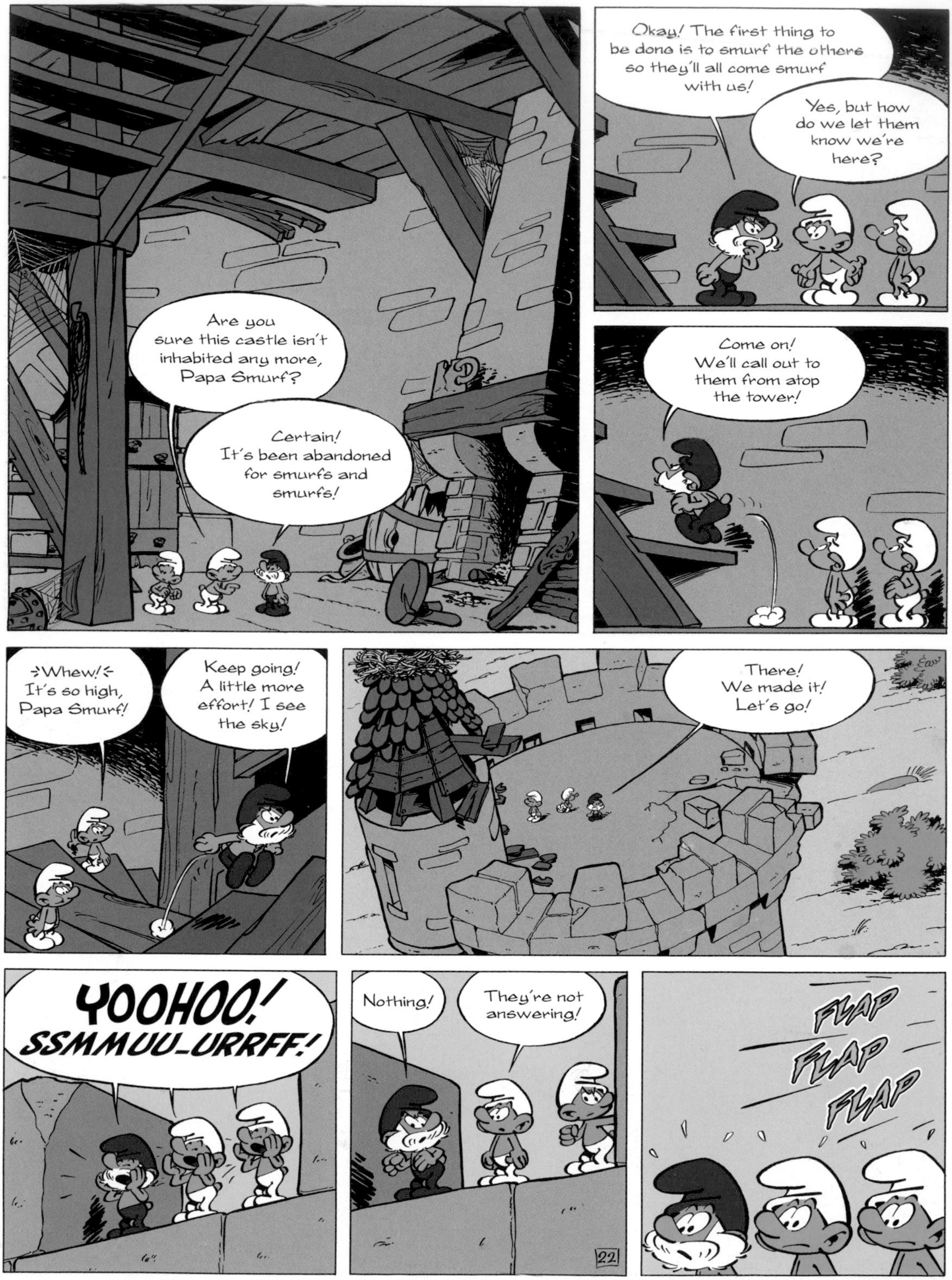
Are you sure this castle isn't inhabited any more, Papa Smurf?
Certain! It's been abandoned for smurfs and smurfs!
Okay! The first thing to be done is to smurf the others so they'll all come smurf with us!
Yes, but how do we let them know we're here?
Come on! We'll call out to them from atop the tower!
Whew! It's so high, Papa Smurf!
Keep going! A little more effort! I see the sky!
There! We made it! Let's go!
YOOHOO! SSMMUU-URRFF!
Nothing!
They're not answering!
22
FLAP FLAP FLAP

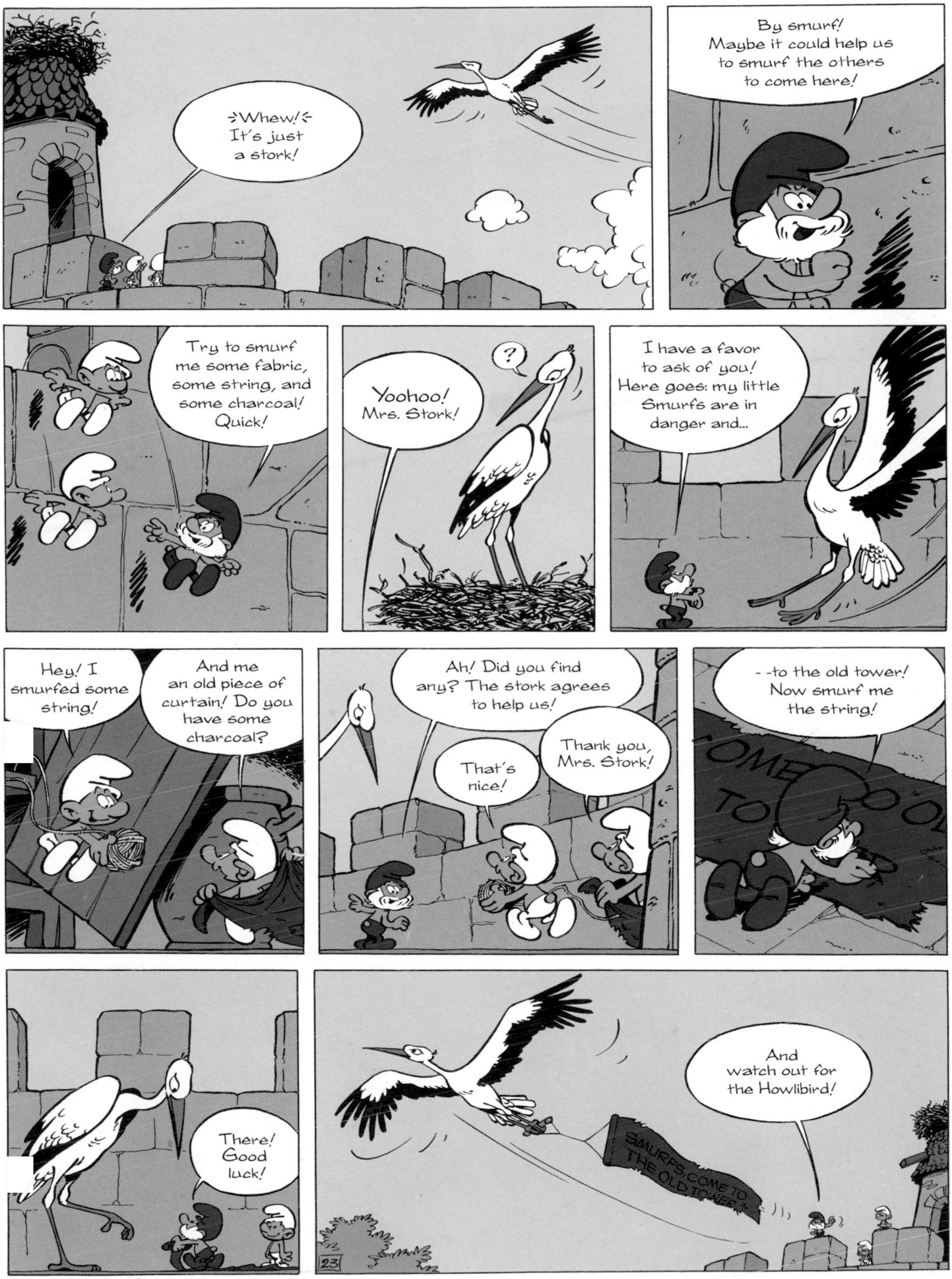

Whew! It's just a stork!
By smurf! Maybe it could help us to smurf the others to come here!
Try to smurf me some fabric, some string, and some charcoal! Quick!
Yoohoo! Mrs. Stork!
?
I have a favor to ask of you! Here goes: my little Smurfs are in danger and...
Hey! I smurfed some string!
And me an old piece of curtain! Do you have some charcoal?
Ah! Did you find any? The stork agrees to help us!
That's nice!
Thank you, Mrs. Stork!
- -to the old tower! Now smurf me the string!
There! Good luck!
SMURFS, COME TO THE OLD TOWER
And watch out for the Howlibird!
23

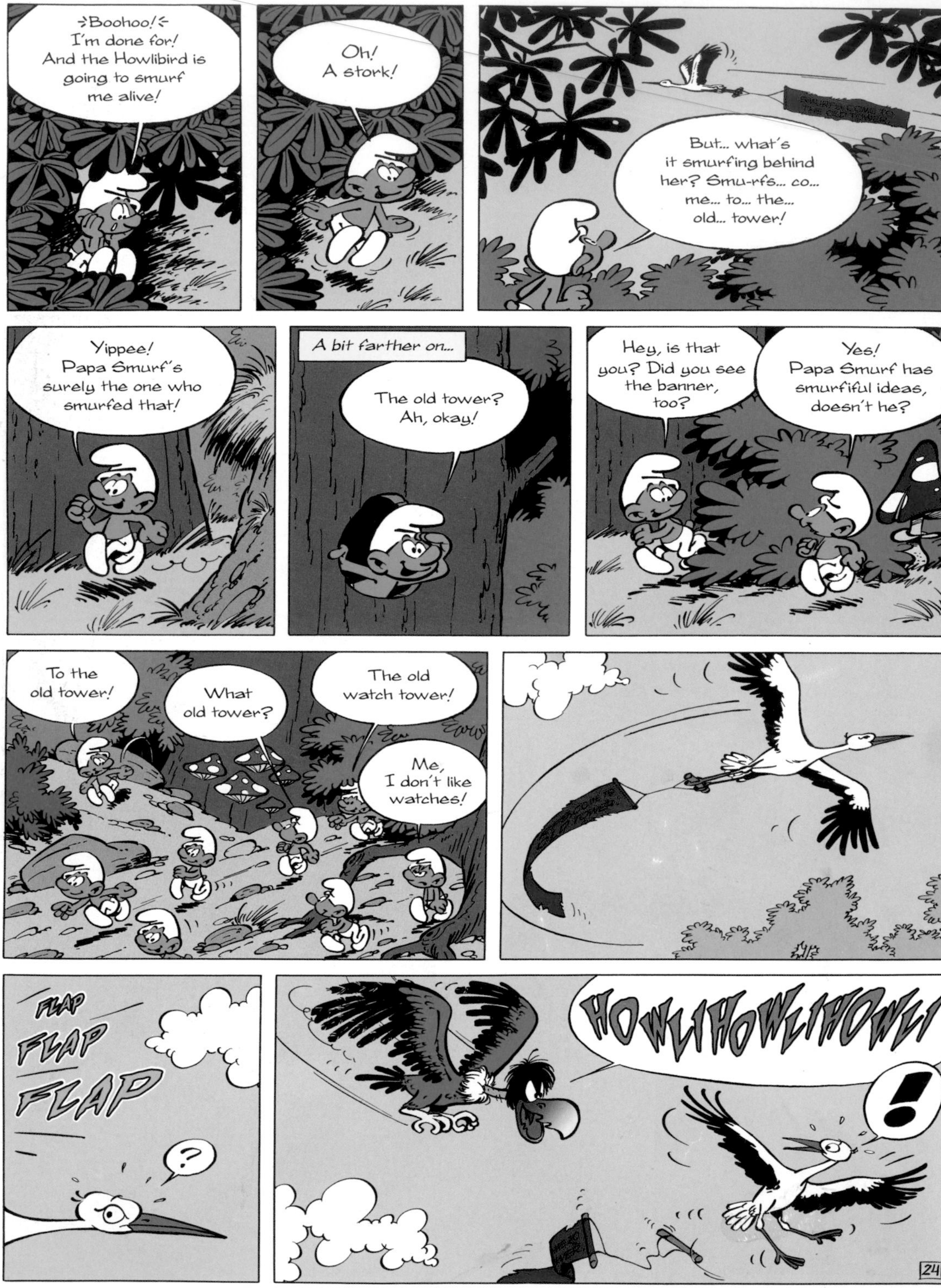

Boohoo! I'm done for! And the Howlibird is going to smurf me alive!
Oh! A stork!
But... what's it smurfing behind her? Smu-rfs... co... me... to... the... old... tower!
Yippee! Papa Smurf's surely the one who smurfed that!
A bit farther on...
The old tower? Ah, okay!
Hey, is that you? Did you see the banner, too?
Yes! Papa Smurf has smurfiful ideas, doesn't he?
To the old tower!
What old tower?
The old watch tower!
Me, I don't like watches!
FLAP
FLAP
FLAP
?
HOWLIHOWLIHOWLI
!
24

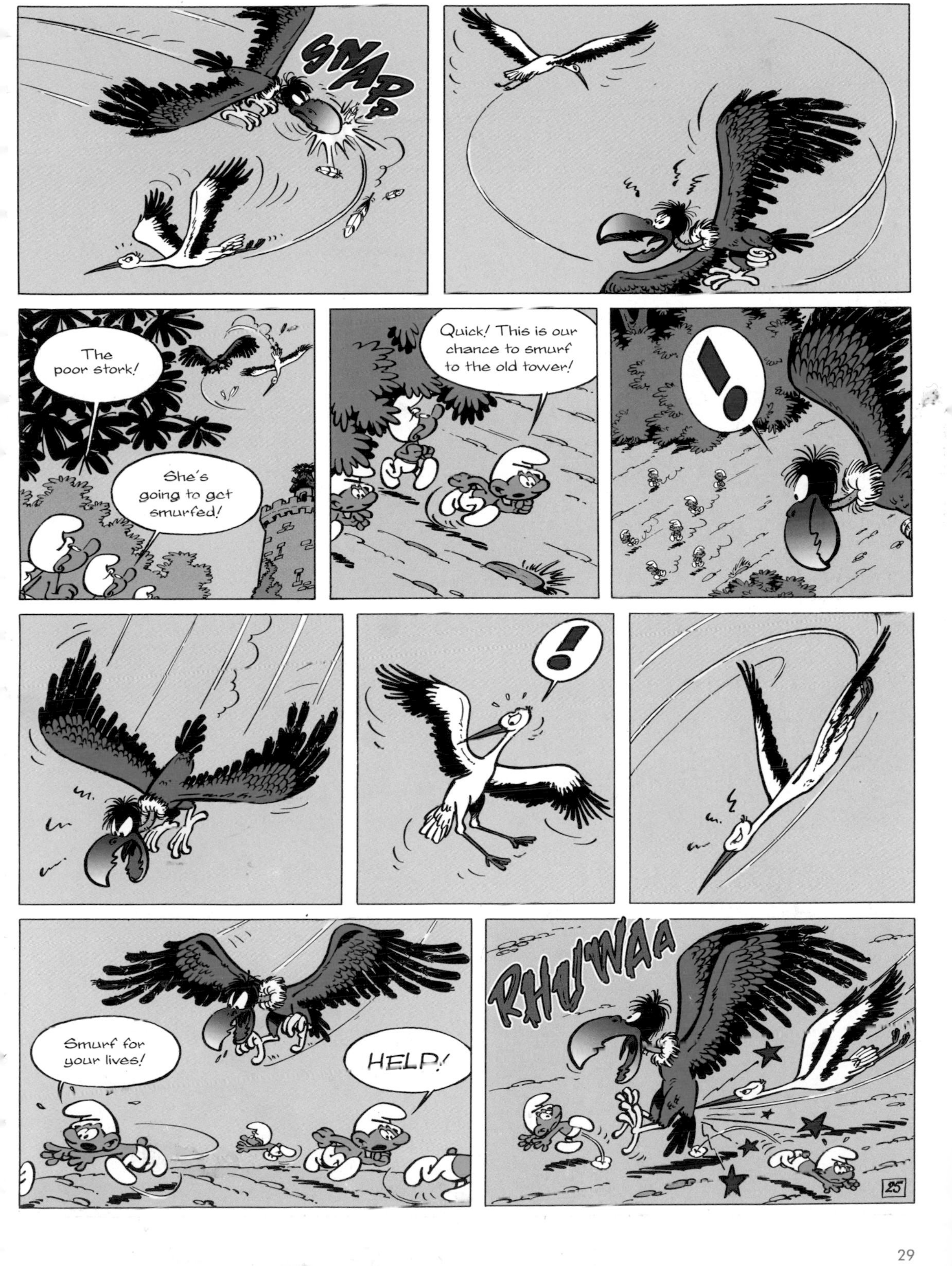
SNAPP
The poor stork!
She's going to get smurfed!
Quick! This is our chance to smurf to the old tower!
!
!
Smurf for your lives!
HELP!
RHUWAA
25

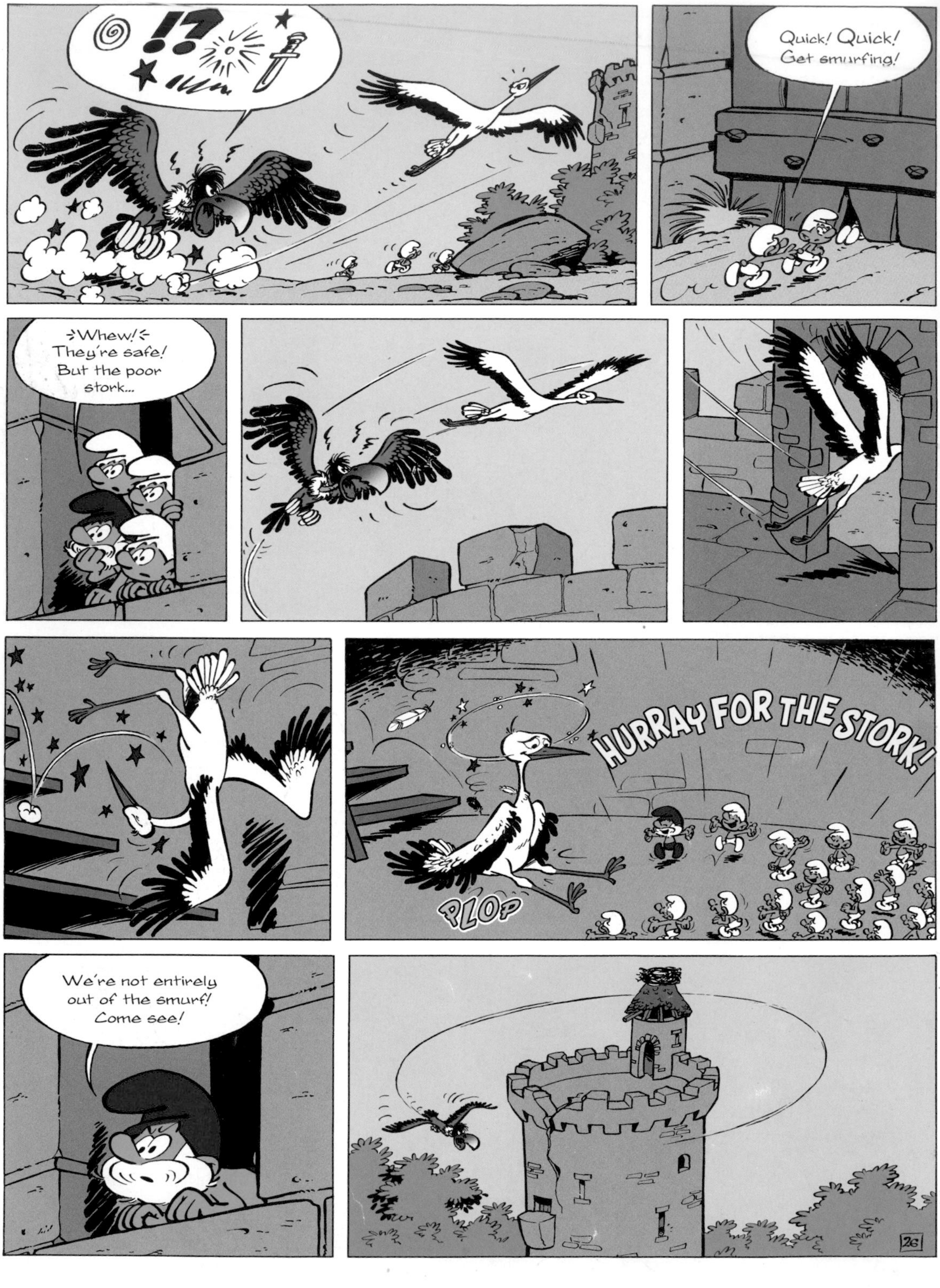
!?
Quick! Quick! Get smurfing!
Whew! They're safe! But the poor stork...
HURRAY FOR THE STORK!
PLOP
We're not entirely out of the smurf! Come see!
26

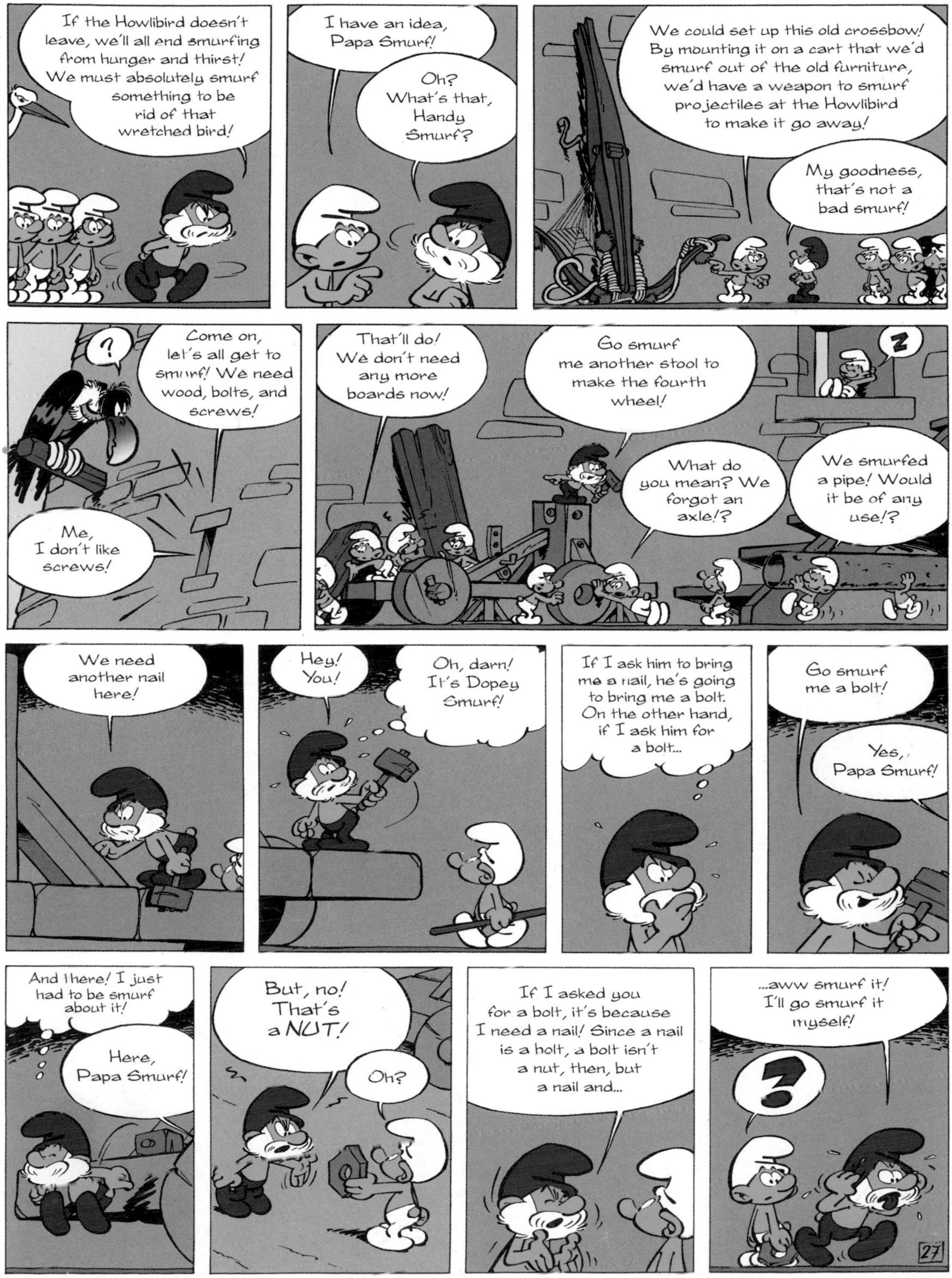
If the Howlibird doesn't leave, we'll all end smurfing from hunger and thirst! We must absolutely smurf something to be rid of that wretched bird!
I have an idea, Papa Smurf!
Oh? What's that, Handy Smurf?
We could set up this old crossbow! By mounting it on a cart that we'd smurf out of the old furniture, we'd have a weapon to smurf projectiles at the Howlibird to make it go away!
My goodness, that's not a bad smurf!
?
Come on, let's all get to smurf! We need wood, bolts, and screws!
Me, I don't like screws!
That'll do! We don't need any more boards now!
Go smurf me another stool to make the fourth wheel!
Z
What do you mean? We forgot an axle!?
We smurfed a pipe! Would it be of any use!?
We need another nail here!
Hey! You!
Oh, darn! It's Dopey Smurf!
If I ask him to bring me a nail, he's going to bring me a bolt. On the other hand, if I ask him for a bolt...
Go smurf me a bolt!
Yes, Papa Smurf!
And there! I just had to be smurf about it!
Here, Papa Smurf!
But, no! That's a NUT!
Oh?
If I asked you for a bolt, it's because I need a nail! Since a nail is a bolt, a bolt isn't a nut, then, but a nail and...
...aww smurf it! I'll go smurf it myself!
?
27

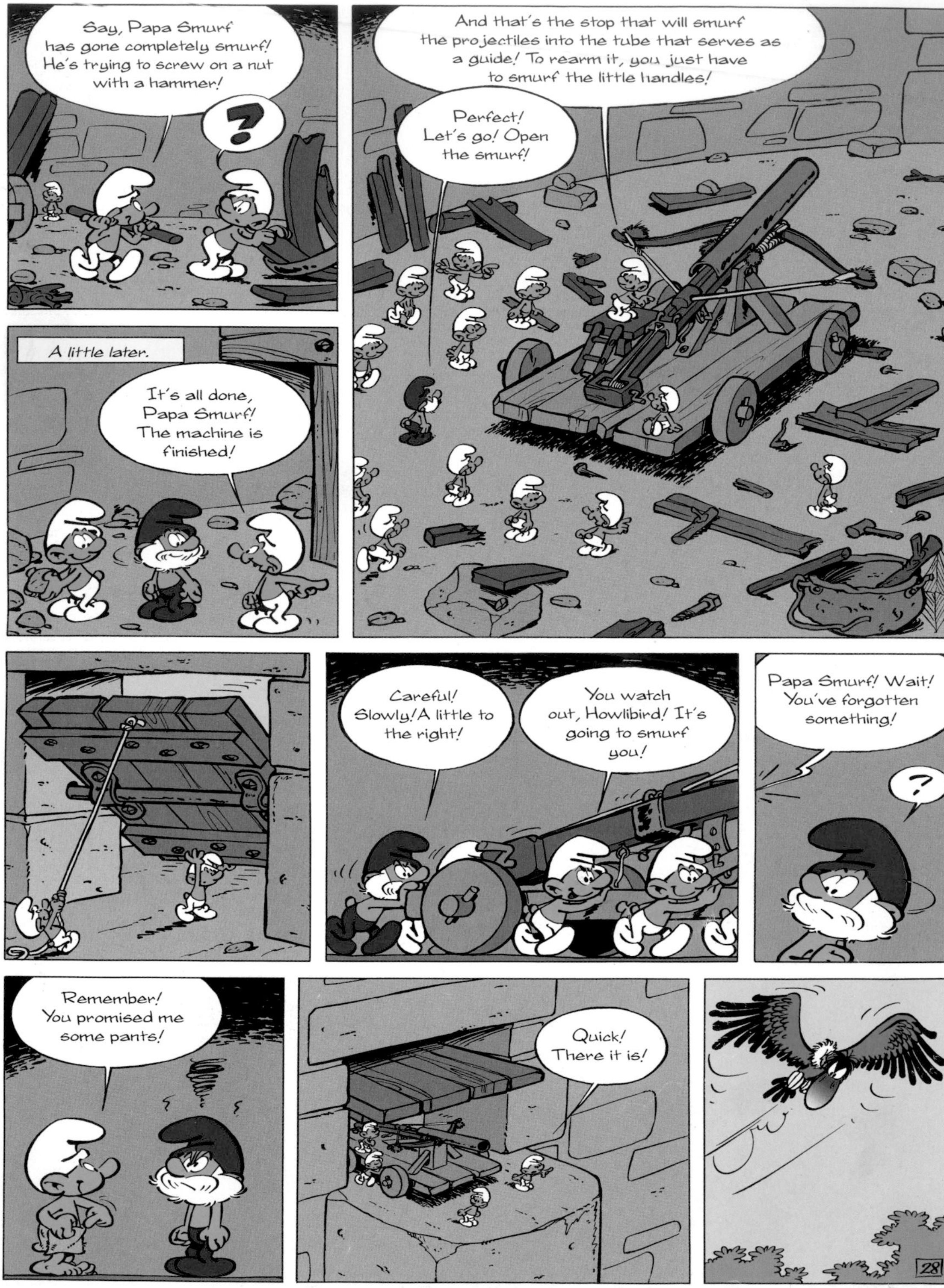
Say, Papa Smurf has gone completely smurf! He's trying to screw on a nut with a hammer!
?
And that's the stop that will smurf the projectiles into the tube that serves as a guide! To rearm it, you just have to smurf the little handles!
Perfect! Let's go! Open the smurf!
A little later.
It's all done, Papa Smurf! The machine is finished!
Careful! Slowly! A little to the right!
You watch out, Howlibird! It's going to smurf you!
Papa Smurf! Wait! You've forgotten something!
?
Remember! You promised me some pants!
Quick! There it is!
28

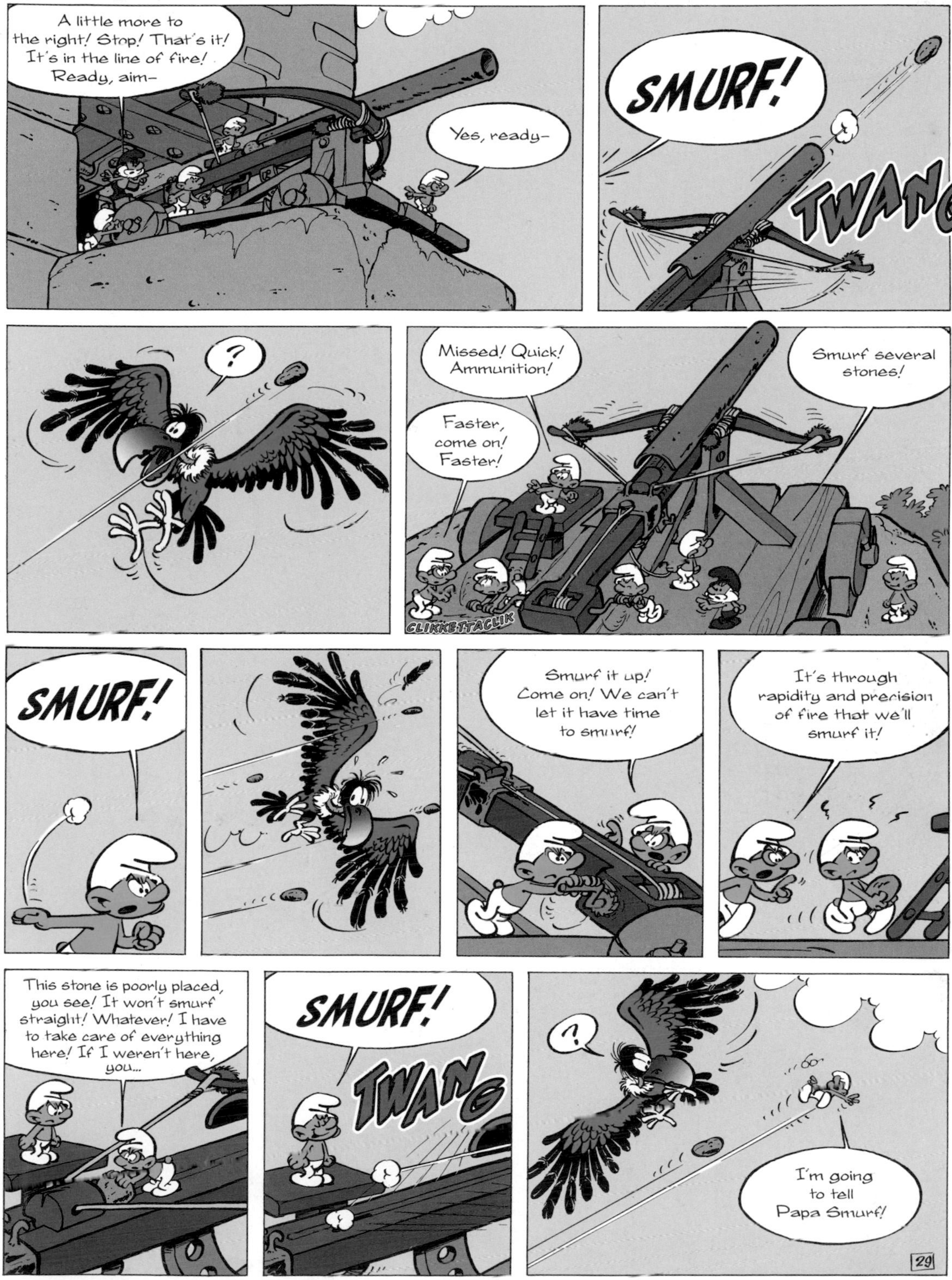
A little more to the right! Stop! That's it! It's in the line of fire! Ready, aim–
Yes, ready–
SMURF!
TWANG
?
Missed! Quick! Ammunition!
Faster, come on! Faster!
Smurf several stones!
CLIKKETTACLIK
SMURF!
Smurf it up! Come on! We can't let it have time to smurf!
It's through rapidity and precision of fire that we'll smurf it!
This stone is poorly placed, you see! It won't smurf straight! Whatever! I have to take care of everything here! If I weren't here, you...
SMURF!
TWANG
?
I'm going to tell Papa Smurf!
29

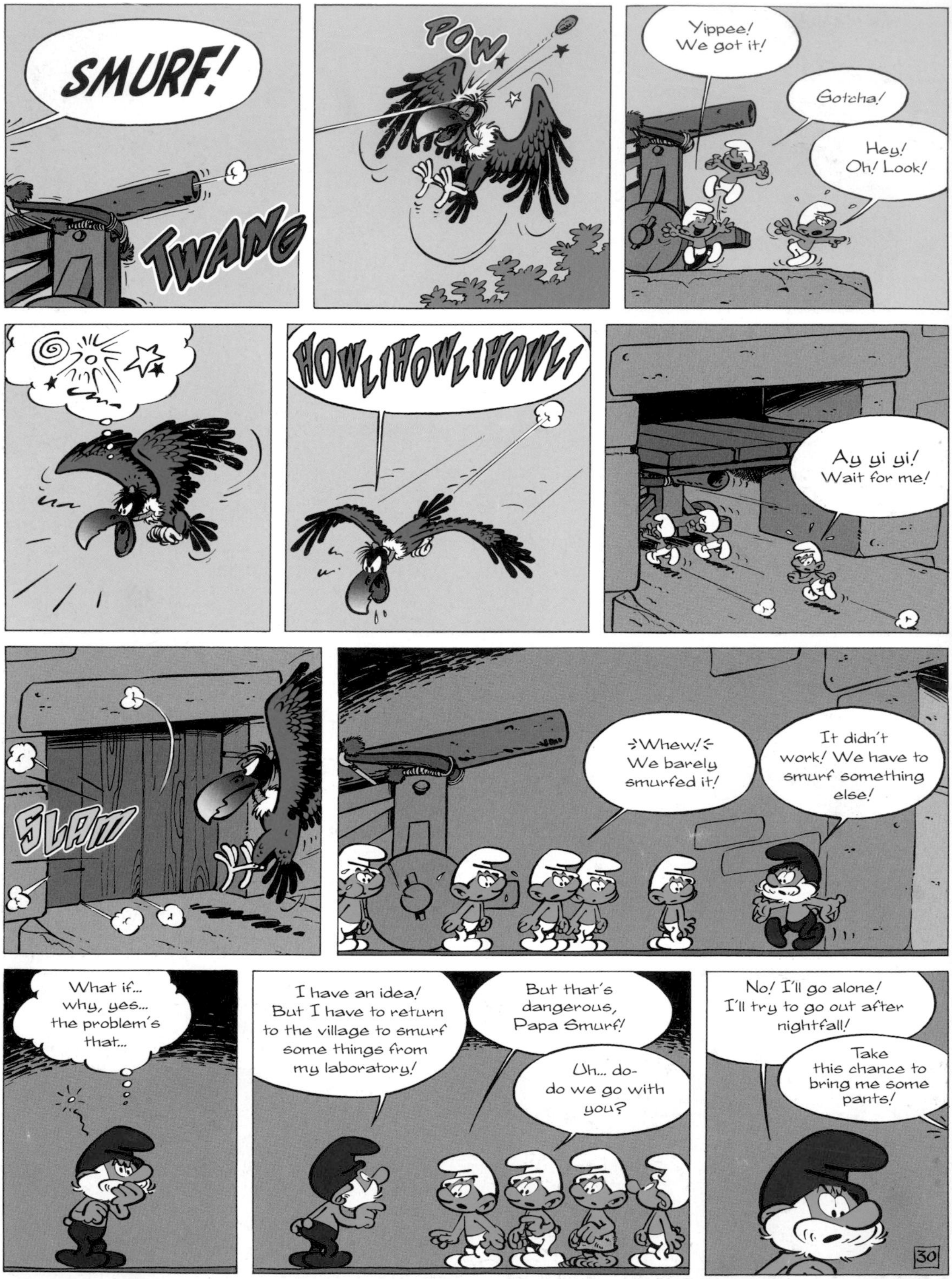
SMURF!
TWANG
POW
Yippee! We got it!
Gotcha!
Hey! Oh! Look!
HOWLIHOWLIHOWLI
Ay yi yi! Wait for me!
SLAM
Whew! We barely smurfed it!
It didn't work! We have to smurf something else!
What if... why, yes... the problem's that...
I have an idea! But I have to return to the village to smurf some things from my laboratory!
But that's dangerous, Papa Smurf!
Uh... do- do we go with you?
No! I'll go alone! I'll try to go out after nightfall!
Take this chance to bring me some pants!
30

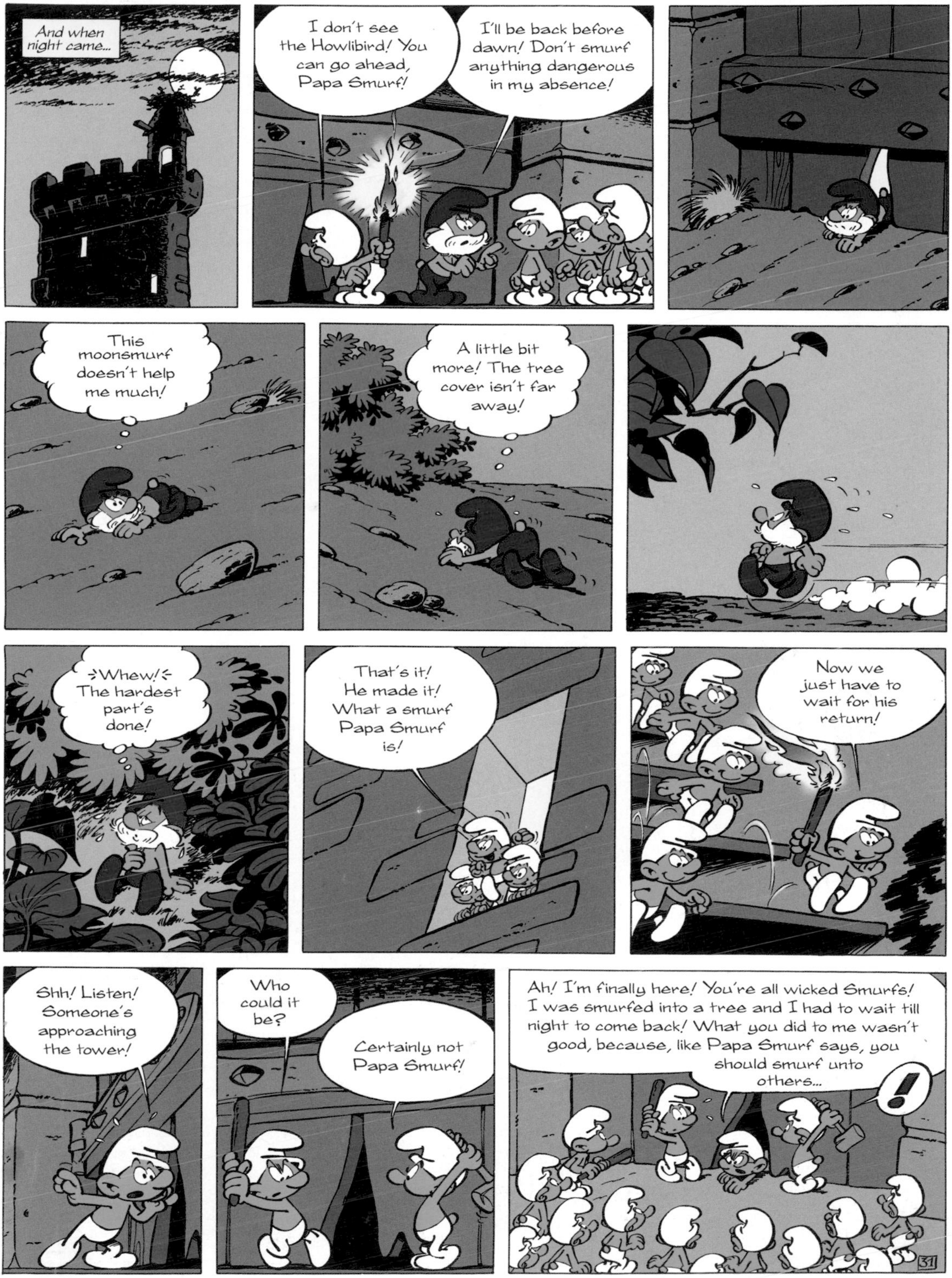
And when night came...
I don't see the Howlibird! You can go ahead, Papa Smurf!
I'll be back before dawn! Don't smurf anything dangerous in my absence!
This moonsmurf doesn't help me much!
A little bit more! The tree cover isn't far away!
Whew! The hardest part's done!
That's it! He made it! What a smurf Papa Smurf is!
Now we just have to wait for his return!
Shh! Listen! Someone's approaching the tower!
Who could it be?
Certainly not Papa Smurf!
Ah! I'm finally here! You're all wicked Smurfs! I was smurfed into a tree and I had to wait till night to come back! What you did to me wasn't good, because, like Papa Smurf says, you should smurf unto others...
!
31

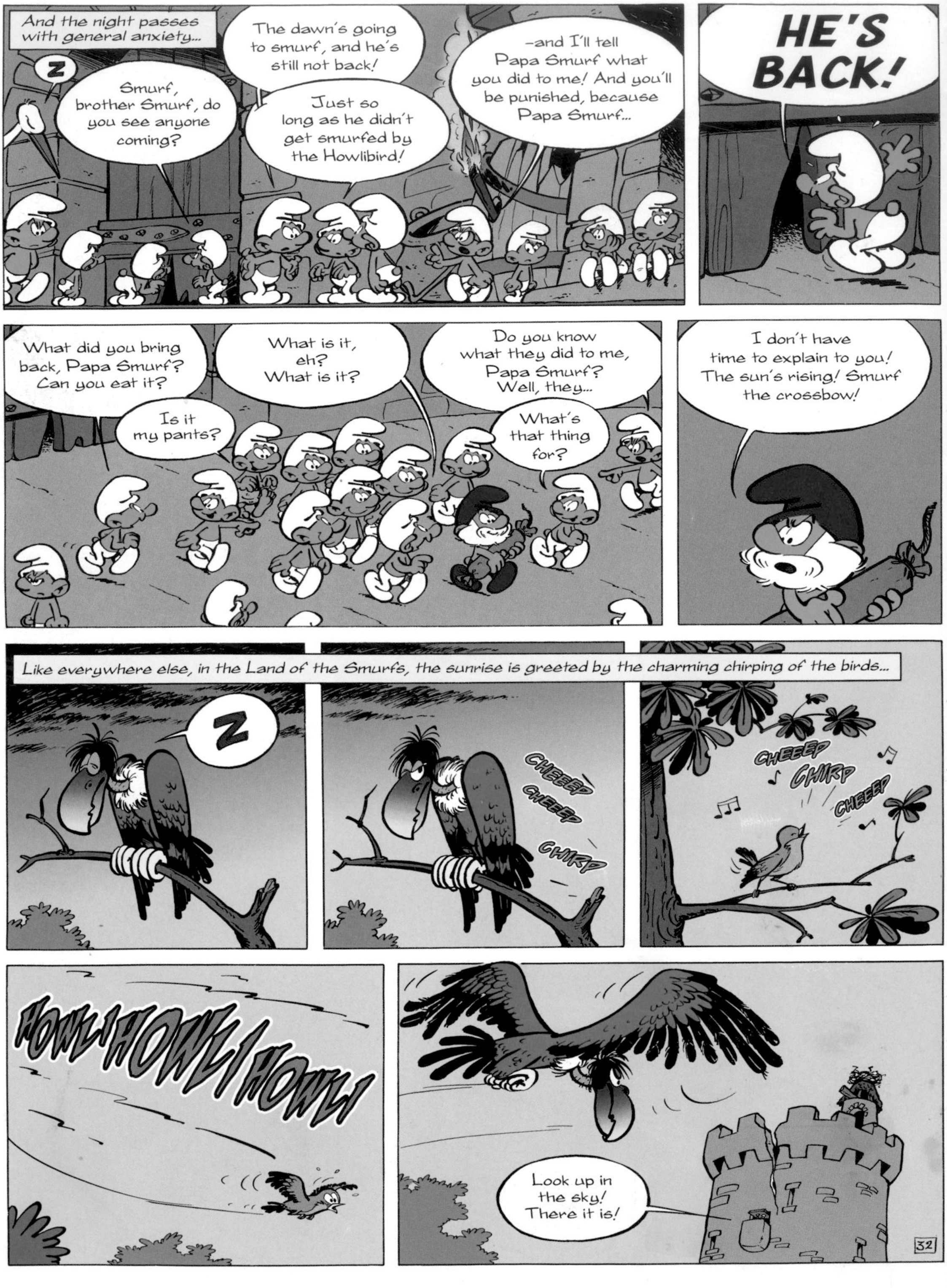
And the night passes with general anxiety...
Z
Smurf, brother Smurf, do you see anyone coming?
The dawn's going to smurf, and he's still not back!
Just so long as he didn't get smurfed by the Howlibird!
–and I'll tell Papa Smurf what you did to me! And you'll be punished, because Papa Smurf...
HE'S BACK!
What did you bring back, Papa Smurf? Can you eat it?
Is it my pants?
What is it, eh? What is it?
Do you know what they did to me, Papa Smurf? Well, they...
What's that thing for?
I don't have time to explain to you! The sun's rising! Smurf the crossbow!
Like everywhere else, in the Land of the Smurfs, the sunrise is greeted by the charming chirping of the birds...
Z
CHEEEP
CHEEEP
CHIRP
CHEEEP
CHIRP
CHEEEP
HOWL! HOWL! HOWL!
Look up in the sky! There it is!
32

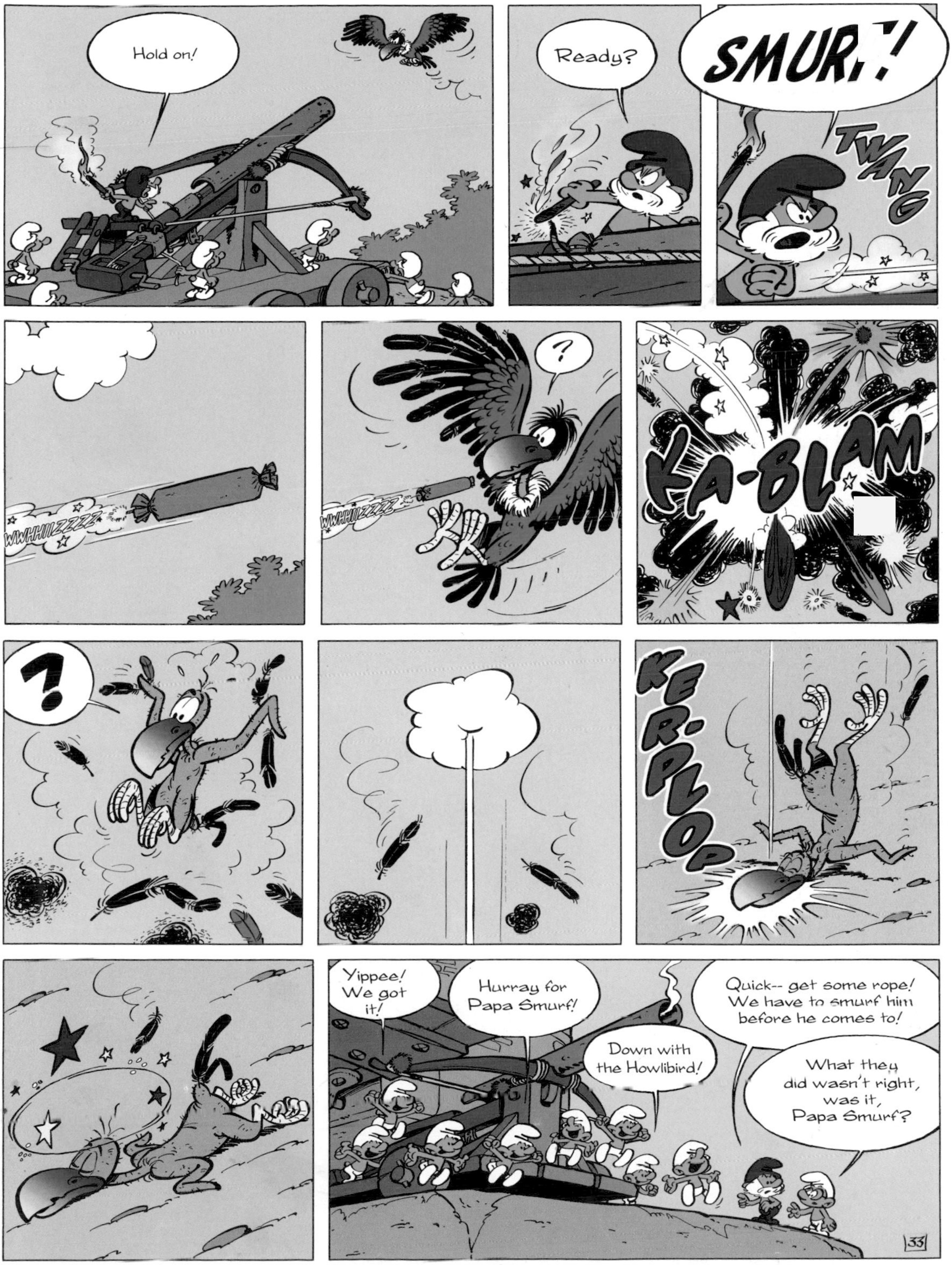
Hold on!
Ready?
SMUR
TWANG
WWHHIIZZZZZ
WWHHIIZZZZZ
?
KA-BLAM
?
KER-PLOP
Yippee! We got it!
Hurray for Papa Smurf!
Down with the Howlibird!
Quick-- get some rope! We have to smurf him before he comes to!
What they did wasn't right, was it, Papa Smurf?
33

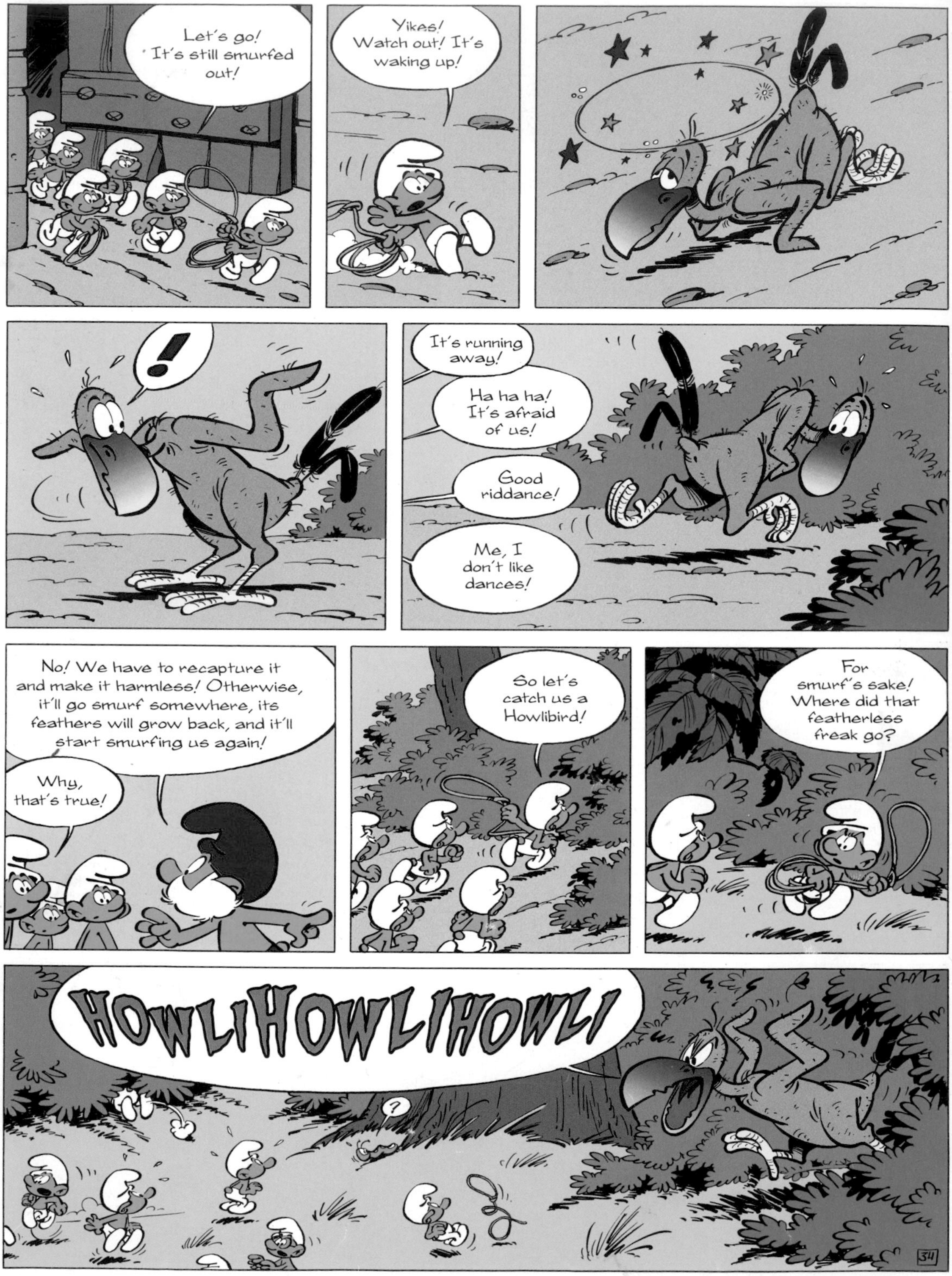
Let's go! It's still smurfed out!
Yikes! Watch out! It's waking up!
!
It's running away!
Ha ha ha! It's afraid of us!
Good riddance!
Me, I don't like dances!
No! We have to recapture it and make it harmless! Otherwise, it'll go smurf somewhere, its feathers will grow back, and it'll start smurfing us again!
Why, that's true!
So let's catch us a Howlibird!
For smurf's sake! Where did that featherless freak go?
HOWLIHOWLIHOWLI
?
34

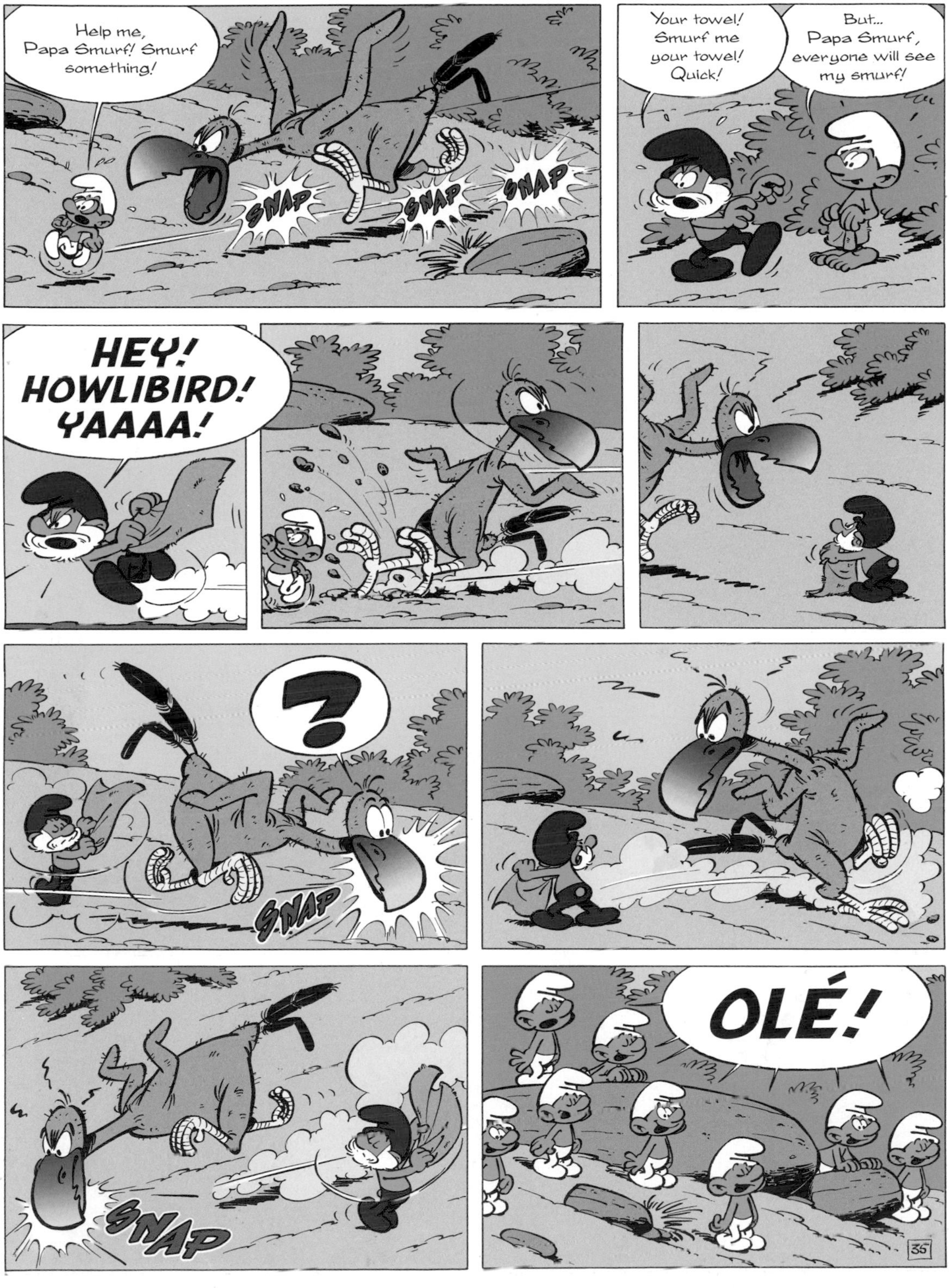
Help me, Papa Smurf! Smurf something!
SNAP
SNAP
SNAP
Your towel! Smurf me your towel! Quick!
But... Papa Smurf, everyone will see my smurf!
HEY! HOWLIBIRD! YAAAA!
?
SNAP
SNAP
OLÉ!
35

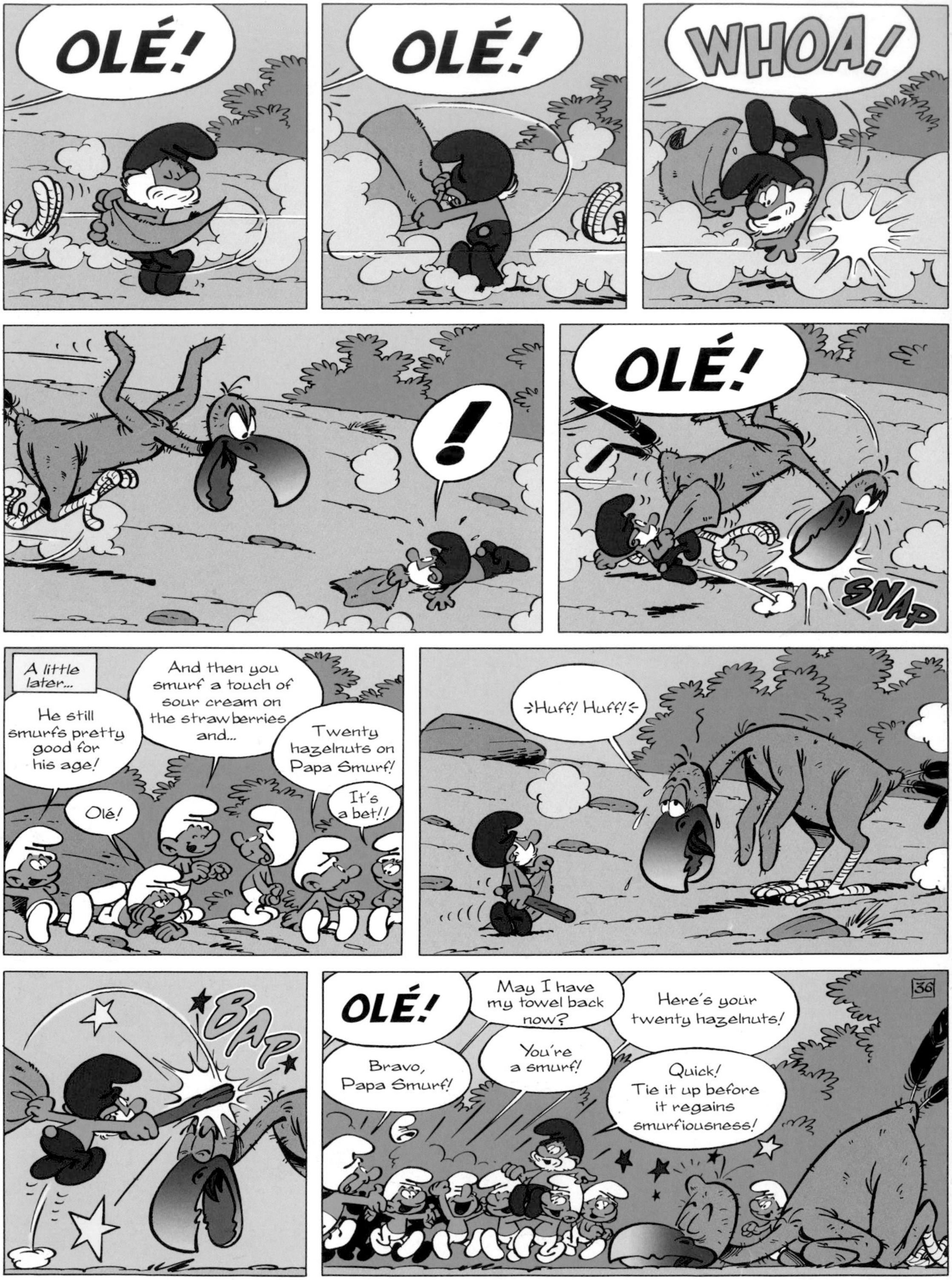
OLÉ!
OLÉ!
WHOA!
!
OLÉ!
SNAP
A little later...
He still smurfs pretty good for his age!
And then you smurf a touch of sour cream on the strawberries and...
Twenty hazelnuts on Papa Smurf!
Olé!
It's a bet!!
-Huff! Huff!-
BAP
OLÉ!
May I have my towel back now?
Here's your twenty hazelnuts!
Bravo, Papa Smurf!
You're a smurf!
Quick! Tie it up before it regains smurfiousness!
36

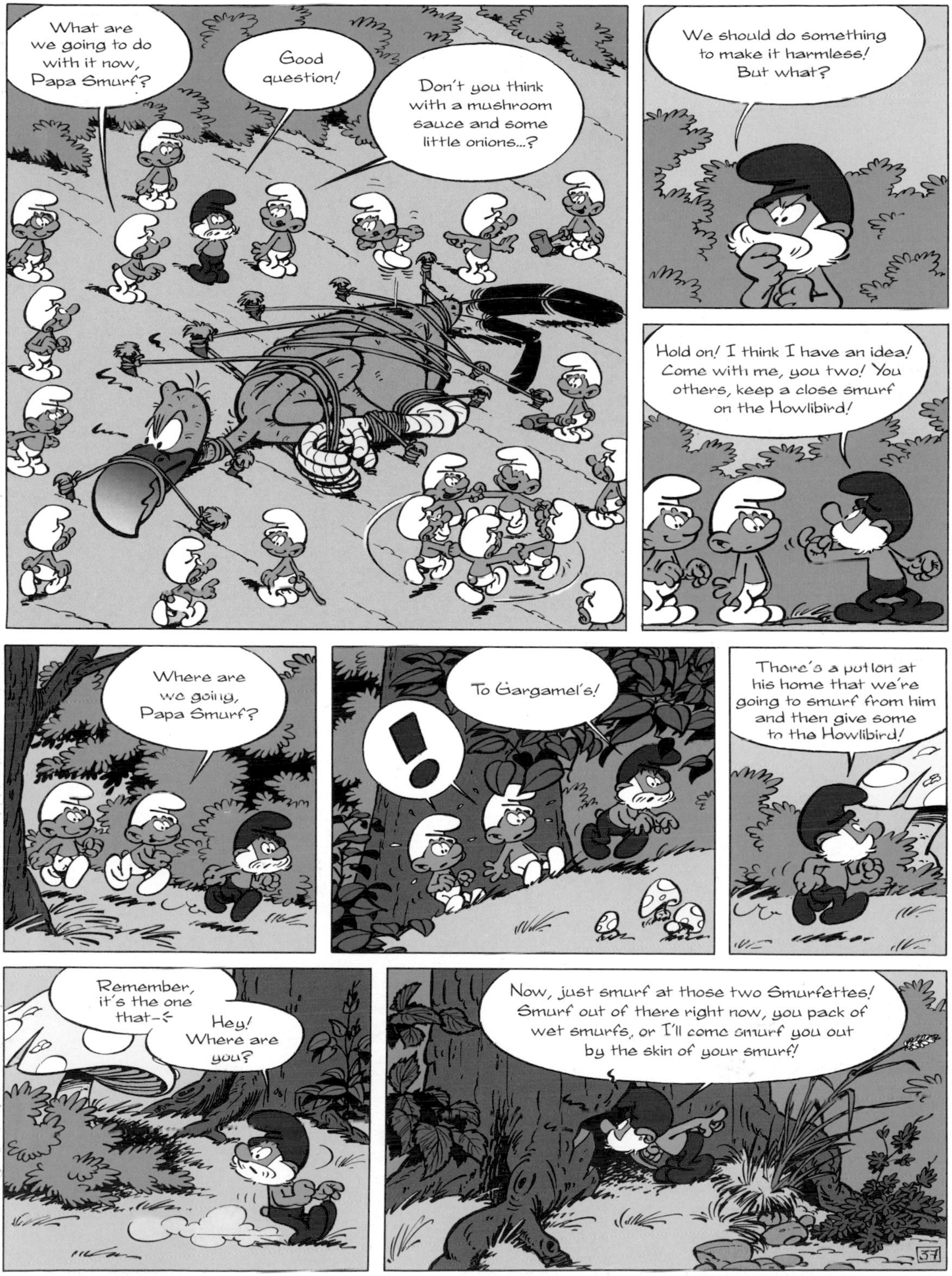
What are we going to do with it now, Papa Smurf?
Good question!
Don't you think with a mushroom sauce and some little onions...?
We should do something to make it harmless! But what?
Hold on! I think I have an idea! Come with me, you two! You others, keep a close smurf on the Howlibird!
Where are we going, Papa Smurf?
To Gargamel's!
!
There's a potion at his home that we're going to smurf from him and then give some to the Howlibird!
Remember, it's the one that-
Hey! Where are you?
Now, just smurf at those two Smurfettes! Smurf out of there right now, you pack of wet smurfs, or I'll come smurf you out by the skin of your smurf!
37

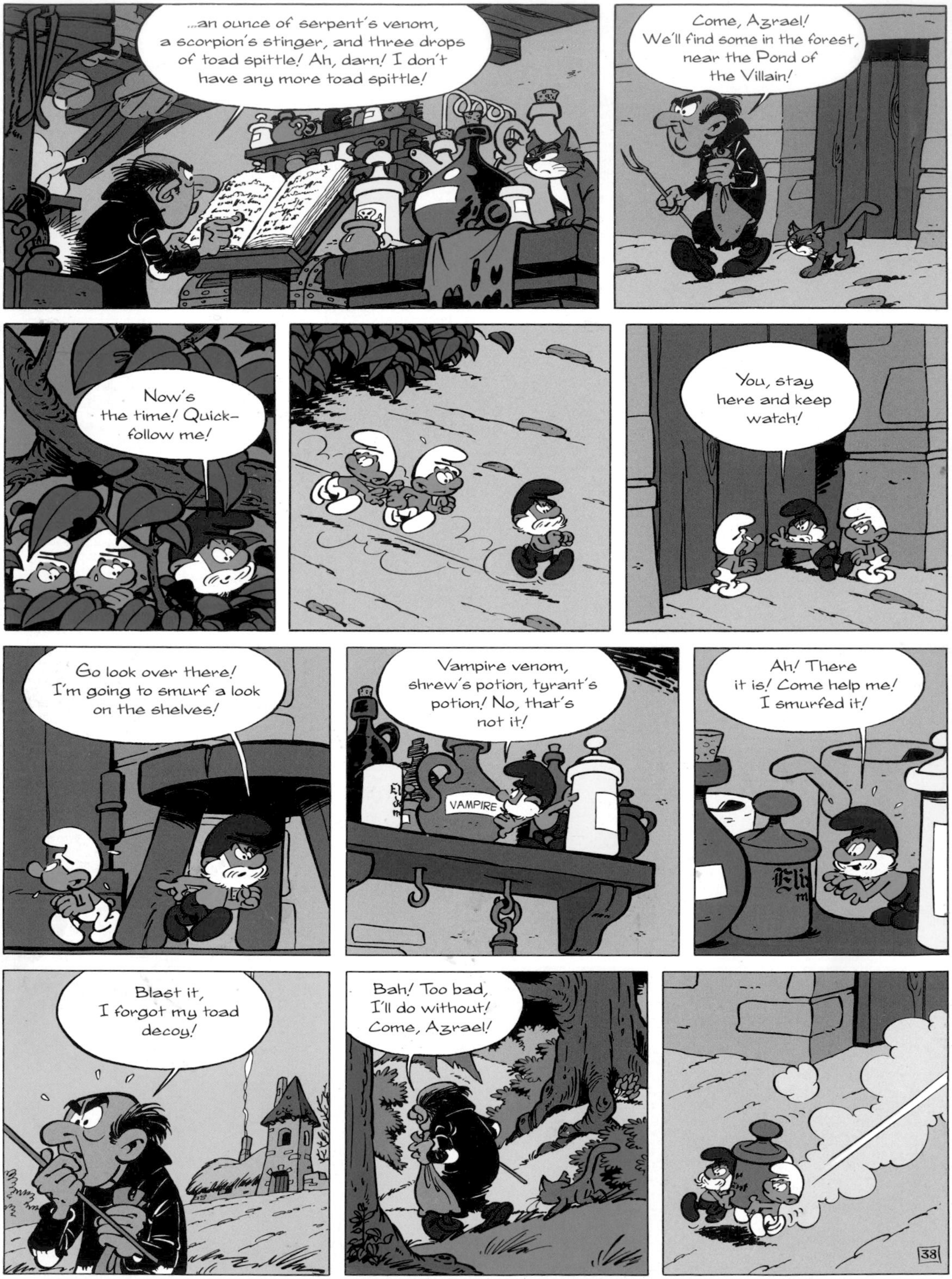

...an ounce of serpent's venom, a scorpion's stinger, and three drops of toad spittle! Ah, darn! I don't have any more toad spittle!
Come, Azrael! We'll find some in the forest, near the Pond of the Villain!
Now's the time! Quick— follow me!
You, stay here and keep watch!
Go look over there! I'm going to smurf a look on the shelves!
Vampire venom, shrew's potion, tyrant's potion! No, that's not it!
VAMPIRE
Ah! There it is! Come help me! I smurfed it!
Blast it, I forgot my toad decoy!
Bah! Too bad, I'll do without! Come, Azrael!
38

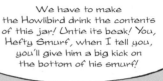

There's Papa Smurf!

What are they bringing with them?

We have to make the Howlibird drink the contents of this jar! Untie its beak! You, Hefty Smurf, when I tell you, you'll give him a big kick on the bottom of his smurf!

Oww!

Hup!

POW

POOF

HA! HA! HA!

But what was in that jar?

Gargamel's famous potion that makes things little! (1)

That's that! Let's return to the village, we've got work waiting for us!

The months pass by. The Smurfs have rebuilt their village.

HOWLI HOWLI HOWLI

?

(1) See "The Smurfnapper" in SMURFS graphic novel #9 "Gargamel and the Smurfs."

43

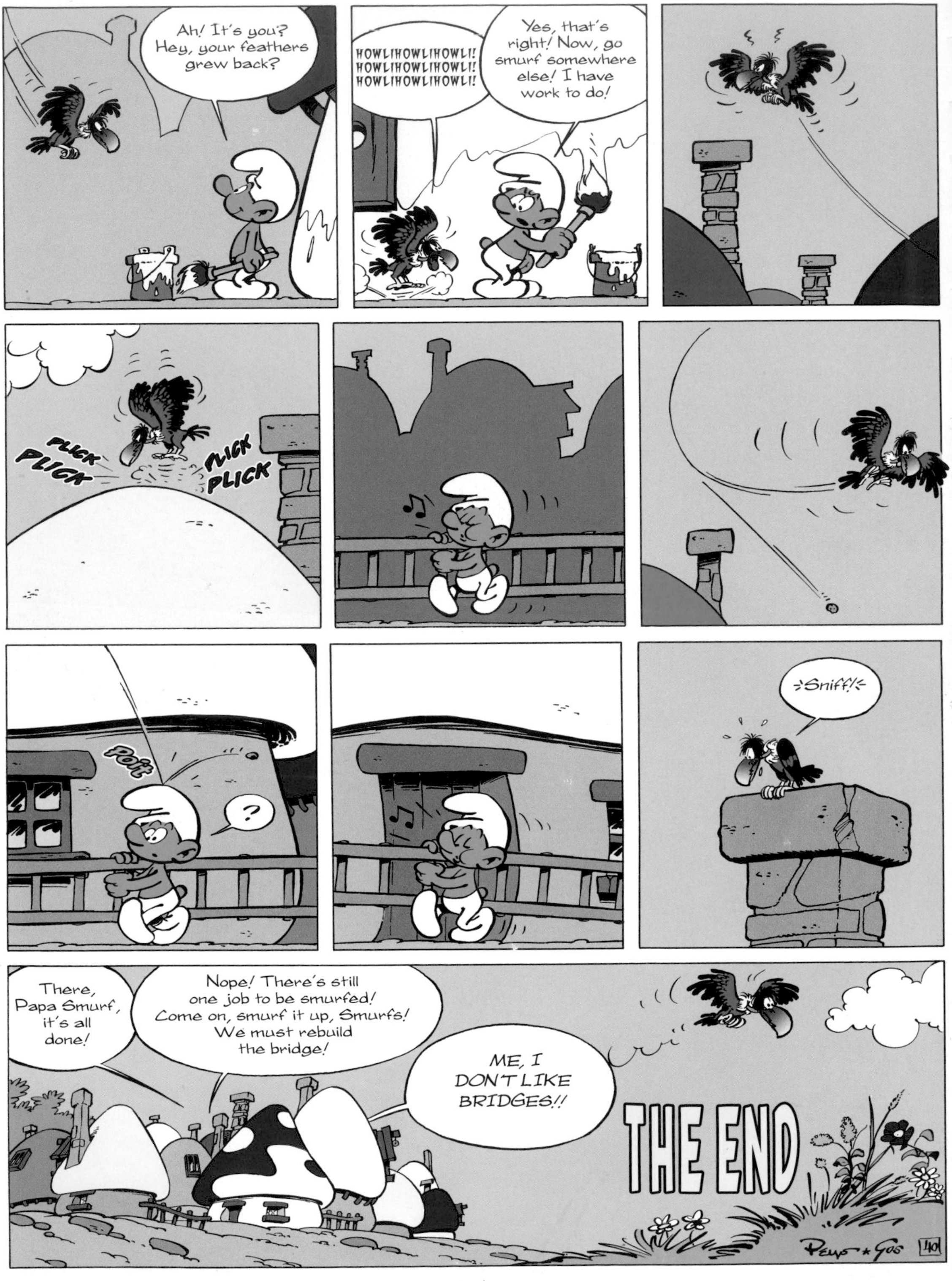

Ah! It's you? Hey, your feathers grew back?
HOWLIHOWLIHOWLI! HOWLIHOWLIHOWLI! HOWLIHOWLIHOWLI!
Yes, that's right! Now, go smurf somewhere else! I have work to do!
PLICK PLICK
PLICK PLICK
Poit
?
-:-Sniff!-:-
There, Papa Smurf, it's all done!
Nope! There's still one job to be smurfed! Come on, smurf it up, Smurfs! We must rebuild the bridge!
ME, I DON'T LIKE BRIDGES!!
THE END
Peyo ★ Gos
40

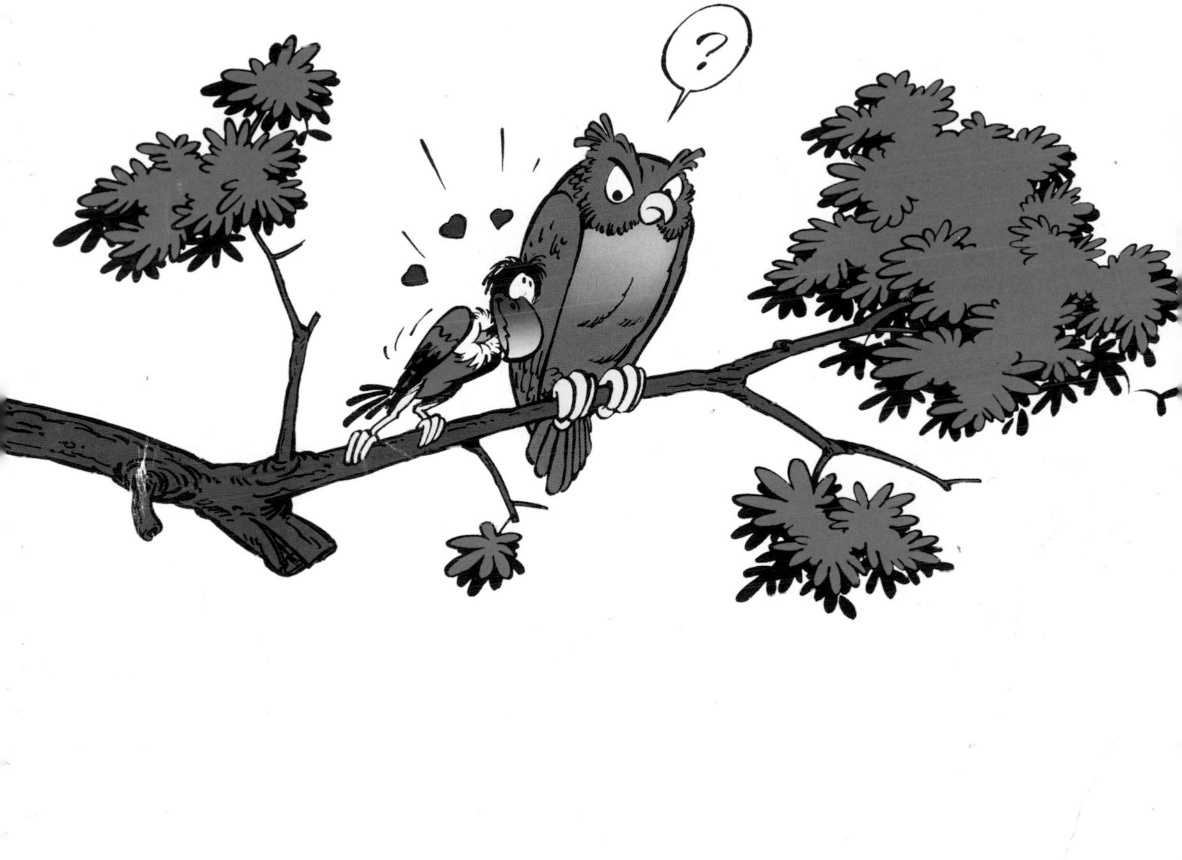
?

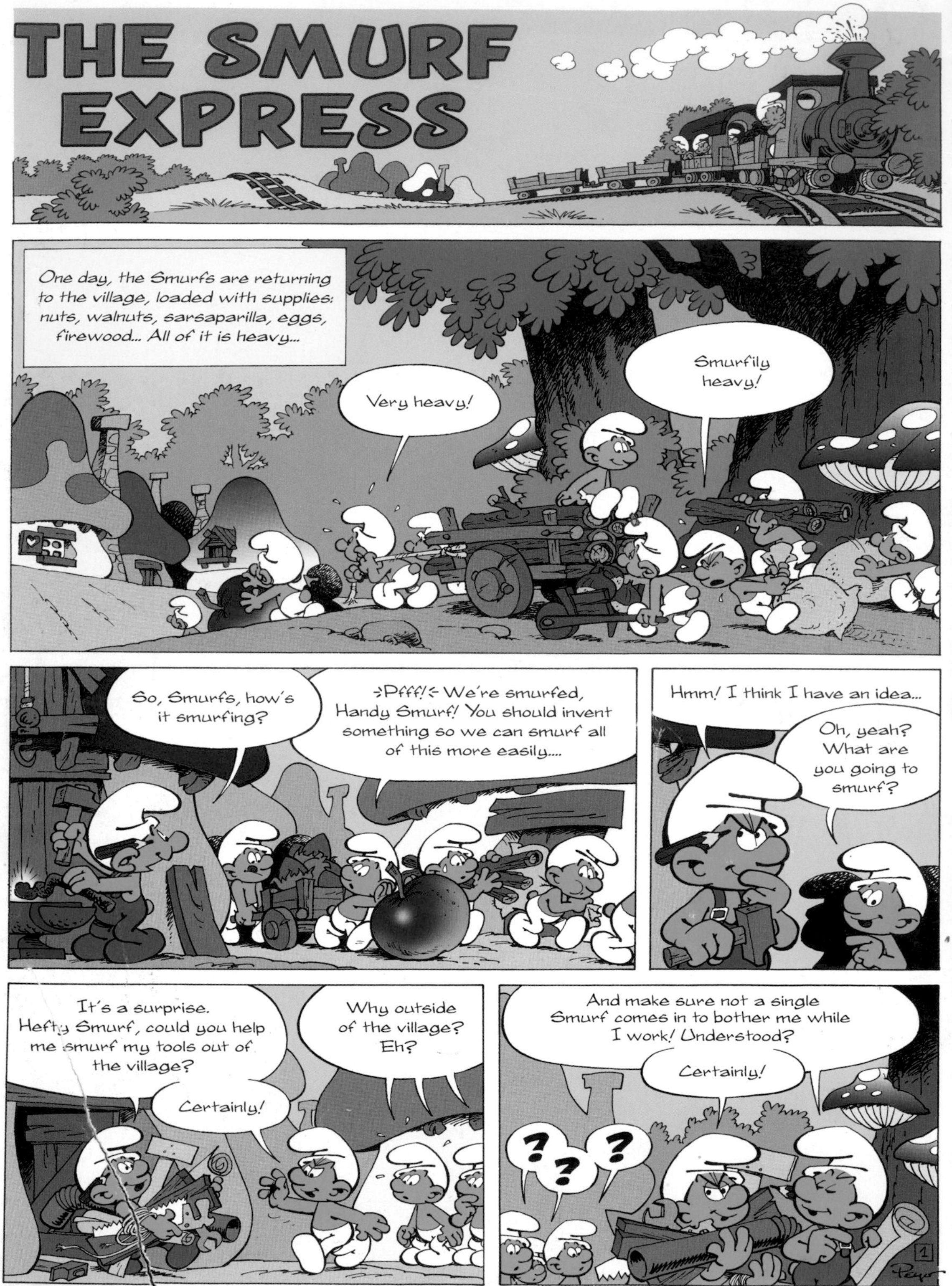
THE SMURF EXPRESS
One day, the Smurfs are returning to the village, loaded with supplies: nuts, walnuts, sarsaparilla, eggs, firewood... All of it is heavy...
Very heavy!
Smurfily heavy!
So, Smurfs, how's it smurfing?
Pfff! We're smurfed, Handy Smurf! You should invent something so we can smurf all of this more easily....
Hmm! I think I have an idea...
Oh, yeah? What are you going to smurf?
It's a surprise. Hefty Smurf, could you help me smurf my tools out of the village?
Certainly!
Why outside of the village? Eh?
And make sure not a single Smurf comes in to bother me while I work! Understood?
Certainly!
? ? ?
1
Peyo

A few days later...

BING BANG BAM

HALT!

STOP!

*BOOM

Uh– it's just us, Hefty Smurf!

We came to see how the work was smurfing along.

IT IS STRICTLY SMURF TO PASS

FORBIDDEN TO SMURF

There's nothing to smurf! Keep moving!

Okay, okay!

FORBID TO SMU

CHOOOO! TOOOOOT!

HURRAY!

I FINISHED! COME, EVERYBODY!

OHHHHH!!

Me, I don't like OHHHHH's!

But what is it?

It's a steam locomosmurf! It smurfs with the driving power of water smurfed into steam by the combustion of wood, which–¿ in short, it's a machine that'll transport the supplies!

It's really besmurfiful...

And smurfily big!

Peyo 2

47

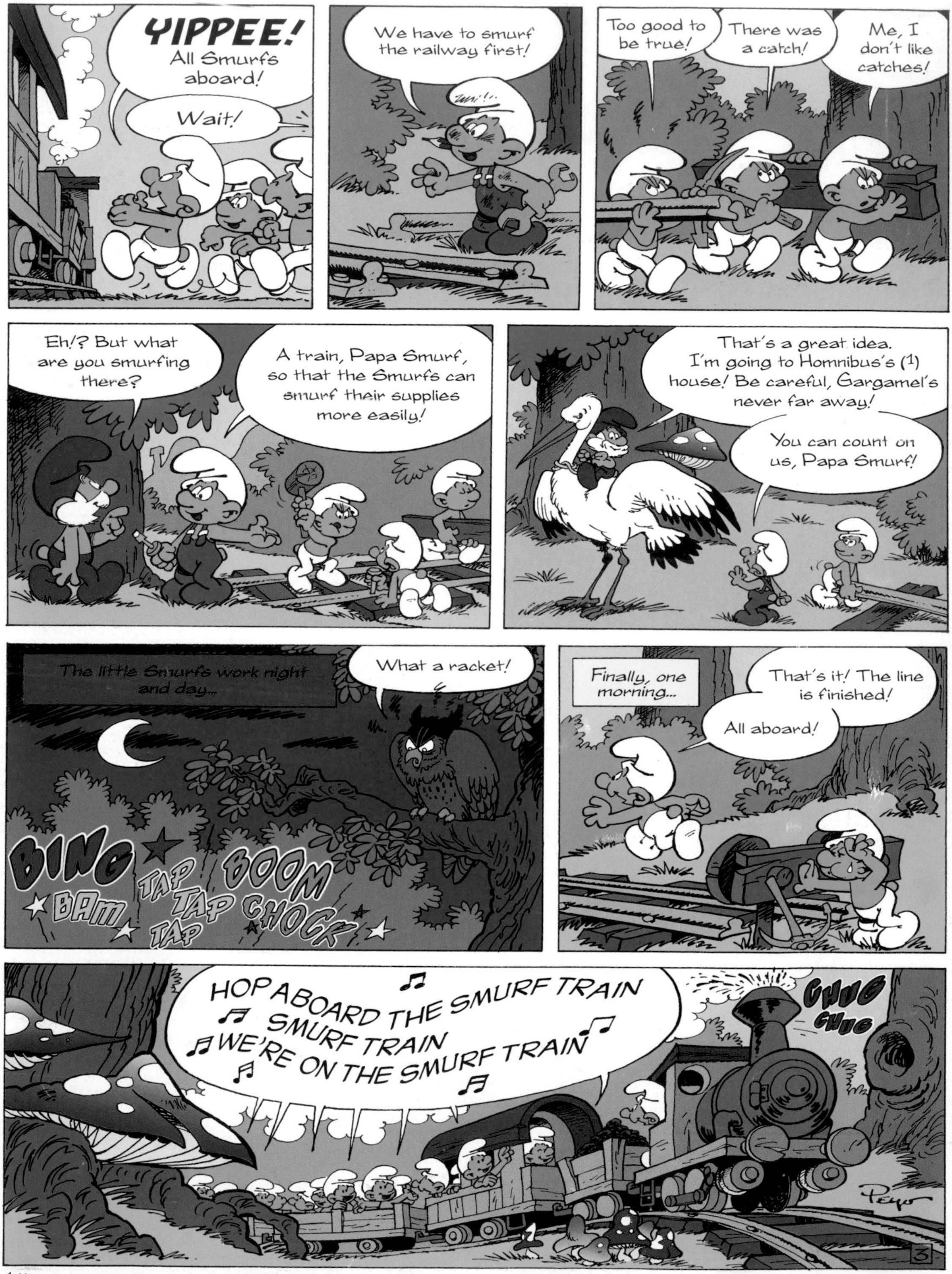
YIPPEE! All Smurfs aboard!
Wait!
We have to smurf the railway first!
Too good to be true!
There was a catch!
Me, I don't like catches!
Eh!? But what are you smurfing there?
A train, Papa Smurf, so that the Smurfs can smurf their supplies more easily!
That's a great idea. I'm going to Homnibus's (1) house! Be careful, Gargamel's never far away!
You can count on us, Papa Smurf!
The little Smurfs work night and day...
What a racket!
BING
BAM
TAP TAP TAP
BOOM
CHOCK
Finally, one morning...
That's it! The line is finished!
All aboard!
HOP ABOARD THE SMURF TRAIN
SMURF TRAIN
WE'RE ON THE SMURF TRAIN
CHUG CHUG
Peyo
3

(1) Homnibus is a friendly wizard. See SMURFS graphic novel#2 "The Smurfs and the Magic Flute!"

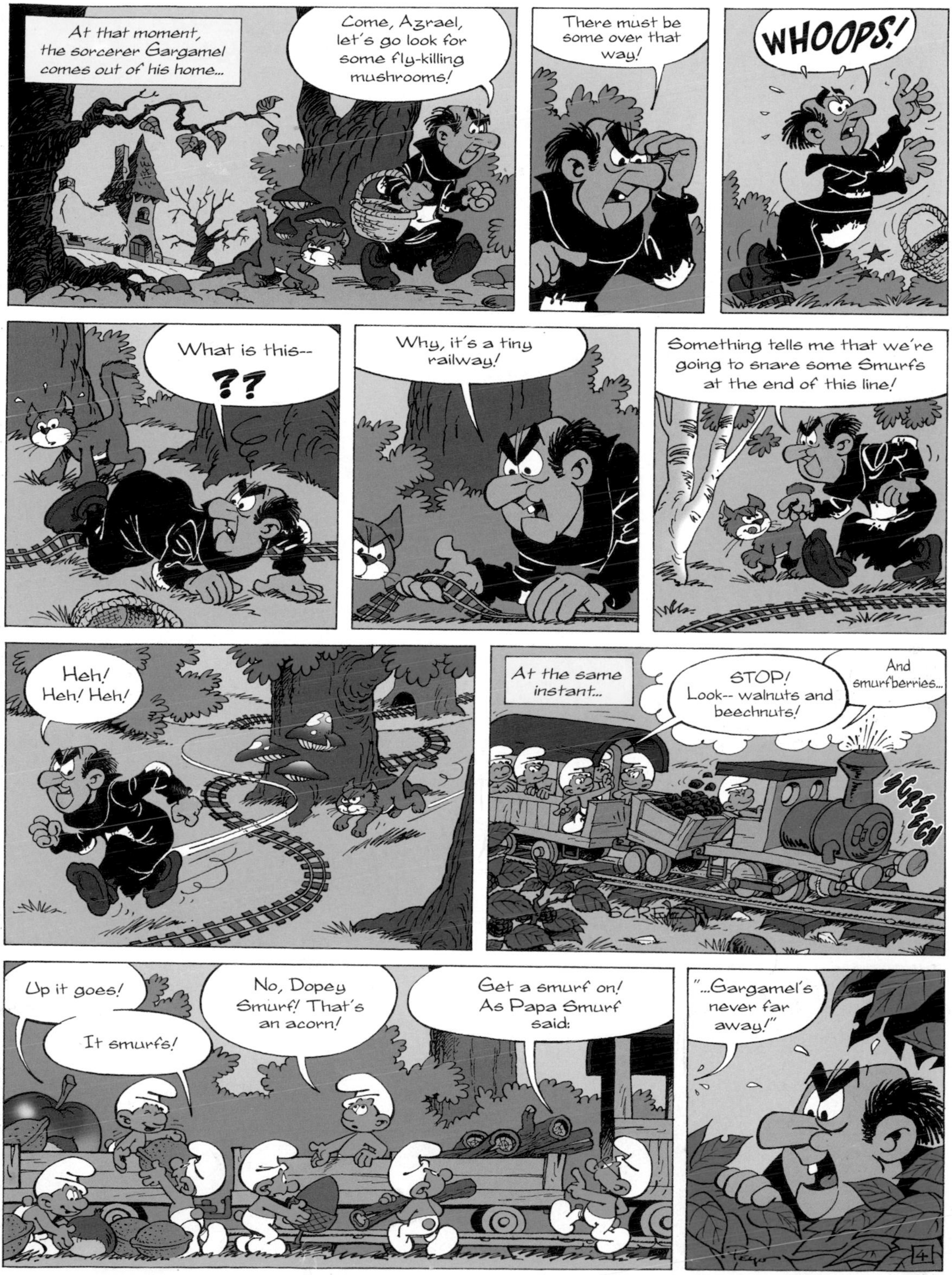

At that moment, the sorcerer Gargamel comes out of his home...
Come, Azrael, let's go look for some fly-killing mushrooms!
There must be some over that way!
WHOOPS!
What is this-- ??
Why, it's a tiny railway!
Something tells me that we're going to snare some Smurfs at the end of this line!
Heh! Heh! Heh!
At the same instant...
STOP! Look-- walnuts and beechnuts!
And smurfberries...
SCREECH
Up it goes!
It smurfs!
No, Dopey Smurf! That's an acorn!
Get a smurf on! As Papa Smurf said:
"...Gargamel's never far away!"
4

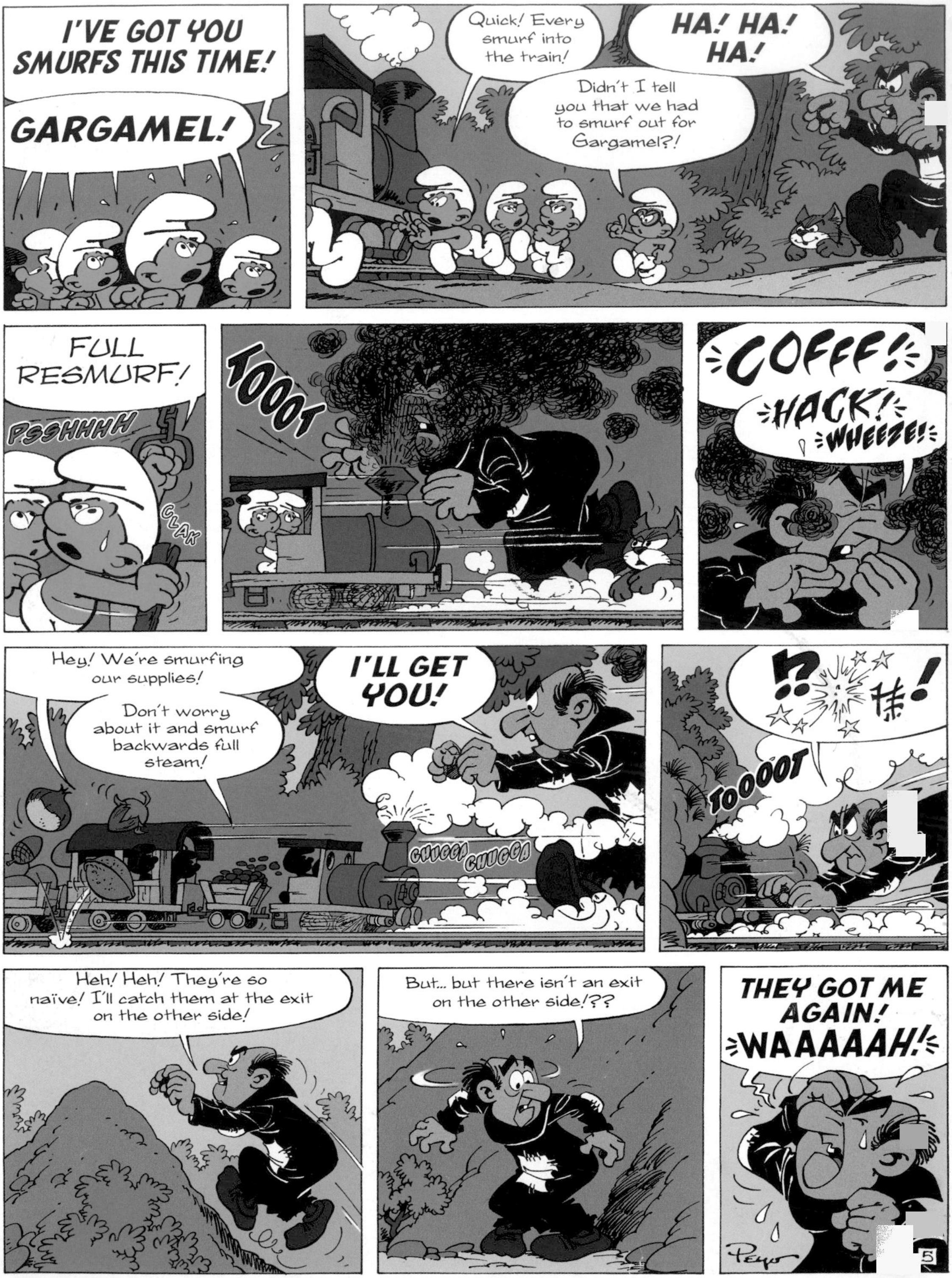
I'VE GOT YOU SMURFS THIS TIME!
GARGAMEL!
Quick! Every smurf into the train!
HA! HA! HA!
Didn't I tell you that we had to smurf out for Gargamel?!
FULL RESMURF!
PSSHHHH
CLAK
TOOOT
COFFF!
HACK!
WHEEZE!
Hey! We're smurfing our supplies!
Don't worry about it and smurf backwards full steam!
I'LL GET YOU!
CHUGGA CHUGGA
TOOOOT
Heh! Heh! They're so naïve! I'll catch them at the exit on the other side!
But... but there isn't an exit on the other side!??
THEY GOT ME AGAIN!
WAAAAAH!
Peyo
5

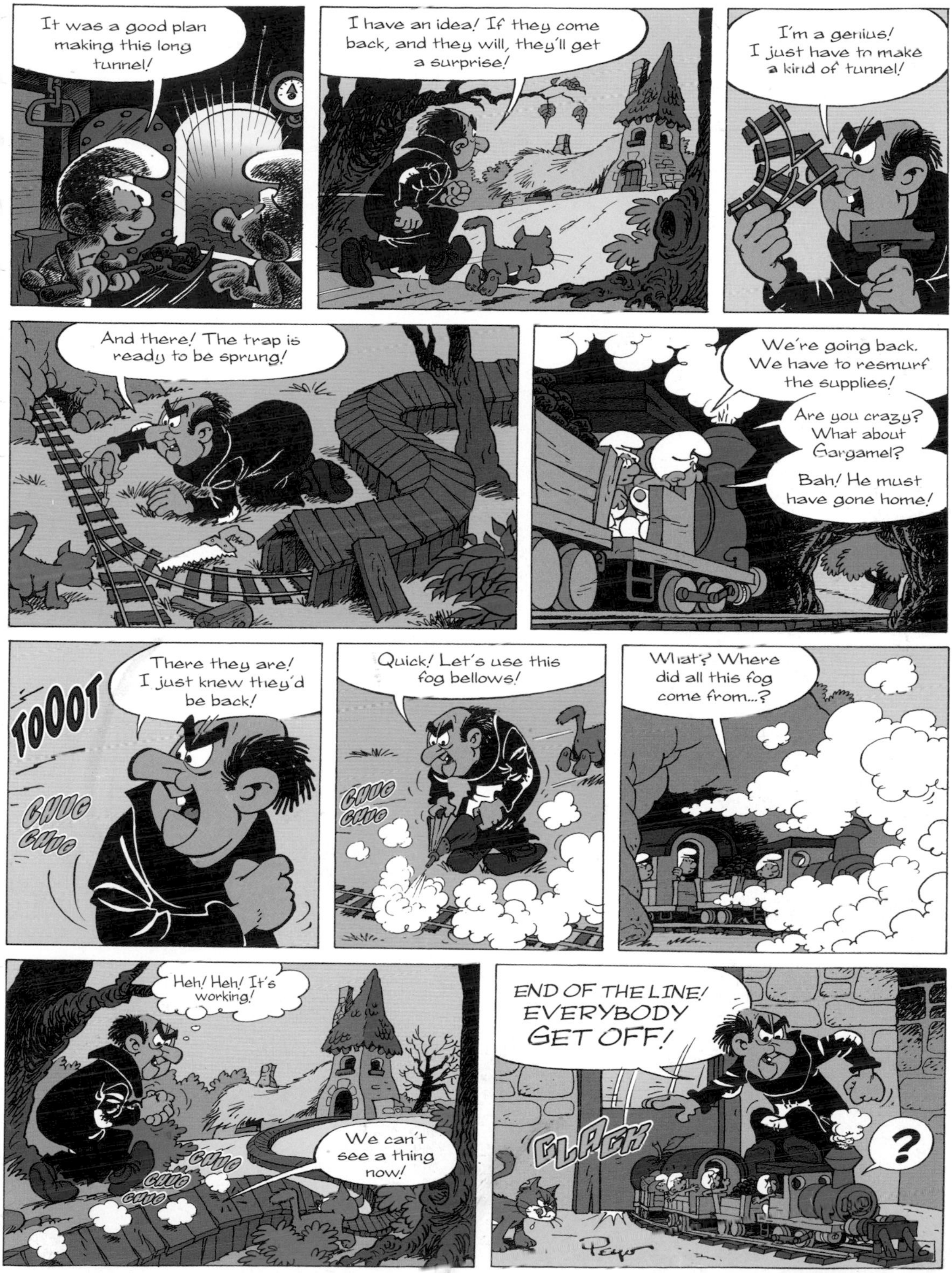
It was a good plan making this long tunnel!
I have an idea! If they come back, and they will, they'll get a surprise!
I'm a genius! I just have to make a kind of tunnel!
And there! The trap is ready to be sprung!
We're going back. We have to resmurf the supplies!
Are you crazy? What about Gargamel?
Bah! He must have gone home!
TOOOT
CHUG CHUG
There they are! I just knew they'd be back!
Quick! Let's use this fog bellows!
CHUG CHUG
What? Where did all this fog come from...?
Heh! Heh! It's working!
CHUG CHUG CHUG
We can't see a thing now!
END OF THE LINE! EVERYBODY GET OFF!
CLACK
?
Peyo

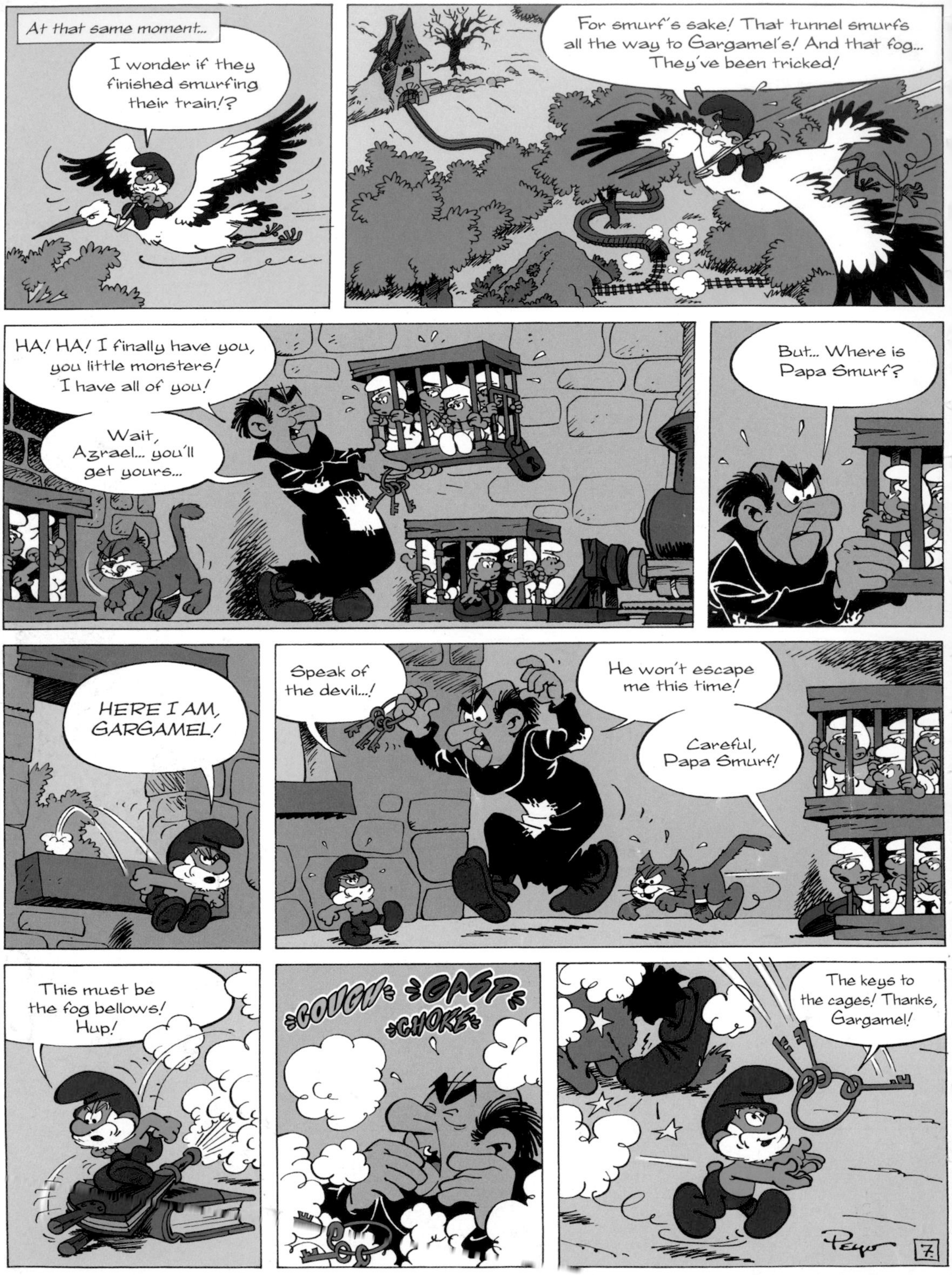
At that same moment...
I wonder if they finished smurfing their train!?
For smurf's sake! That tunnel smurfs all the way to Gargamel's! And that fog... They've been tricked!
HA! HA! I finally have you, you little monsters! I have all of you!
Wait, Azrael... you'll get yours...
But... Where is Papa Smurf?
HERE I AM, GARGAMEL!
Speak of the devil...!
He won't escape me this time!
Careful, Papa Smurf!
This must be the fog bellows! Hup!
COUGH
GASP
CHOKE
The keys to the cages! Thanks, Gargamel!
Peyo
7.

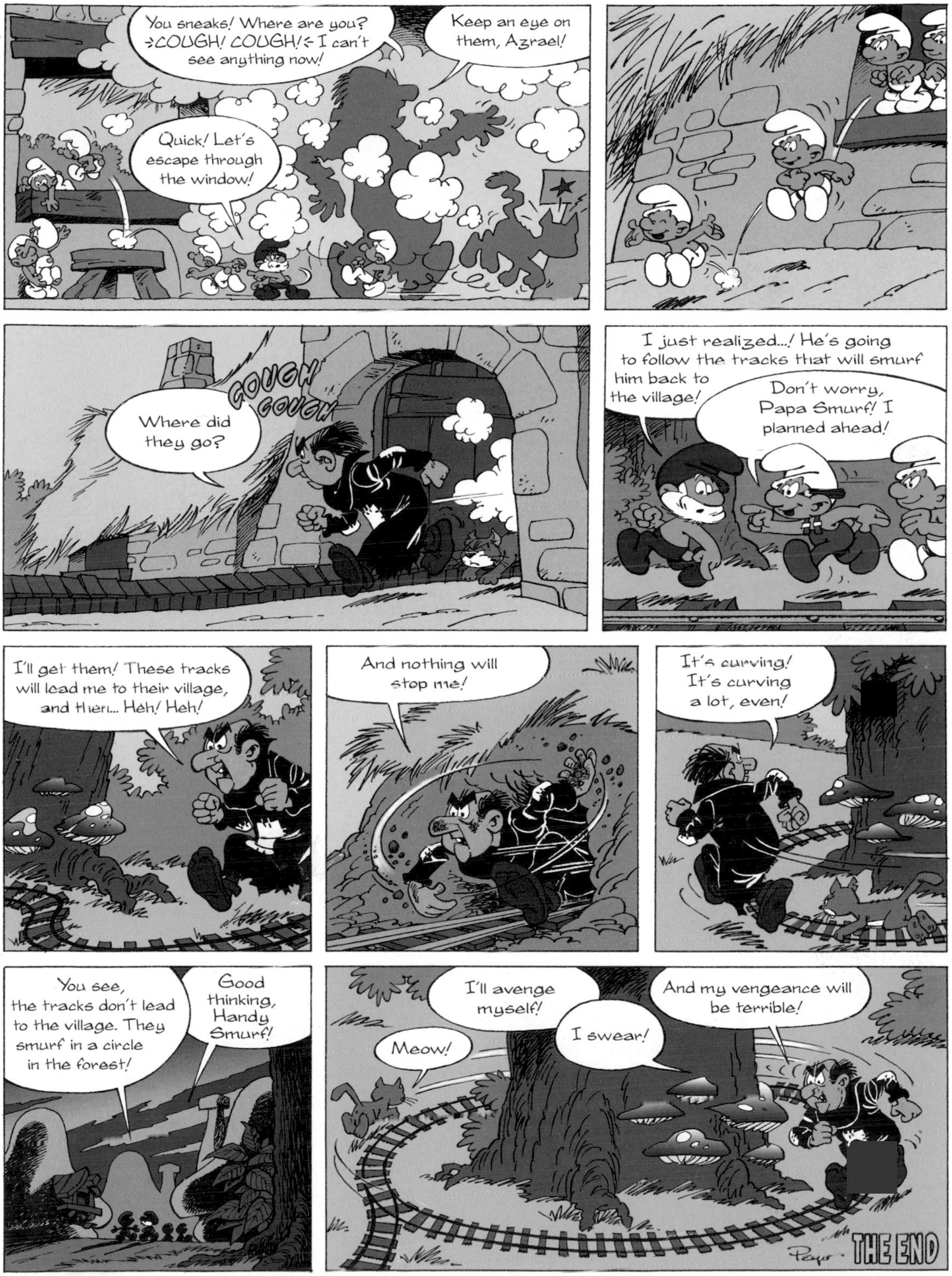
You sneaks! Where are you? →COUGH! COUGH!← I can't see anything now!
Keep an eye on them, Azrael!
Quick! Let's escape through the window!
COUGH COUGH
Where did they go?
I just realized...! He's going to follow the tracks that will smurf him back to the village!
Don't worry, Papa Smurf! I planned ahead!
I'll get them! These tracks will lead me to their village, and then... Heh! Heh!
And nothing will stop me!
It's curving! It's curving a lot, even!
You see, the tracks don't lead to the village. They smurf in a circle in the forest!
Good thinking, Handy Smurf!
I'll avenge myself!
Meow!
I swear!
And my vengeance will be terrible!
Peyo
THE END

WATCH OUT FOR PAPERCUTZ™

Welcome to the sixth SMURFS graphic novel from Papercutz, the little graphic novel publisher featuring the biggest stars. I'm Jim Salicrup, the Smurf-in-Chief, and I'm betting that I'm as super-excited as you and Smurfs-fans everywhere are about this year's unbelievable smurf-happenings.

The biggest event has to be the August 3rd opening of the all-new, big-budget Smurfs movie. It's the very first time the Smurfs will be appearing in a live-action movie, and the first time the Smurfs will be computer-animated and in 3D. The Columbia/Sony movie stars Hank Azaria (as Gargamel), Neil Patrick Harris, and the voices of Katy Perry (as the Smurfette), Paul Reubens (as Jokey Smurf), B.J. Novak (as Baker Smurf), Jonathan Winters (as Papa Smurf), George Lopez (as Grouchy Smurf), and many more. For more information on the Smurfiest movie ever, just go to www.smurfhappens.com

Of course, for fans of the Smurfs animated Hanna-Barbera TV series, the first two seasons are available on DVD from Warner Home Video. (In the later seasons, Jonathan Winters supplied the voice to Grandpa Smurf—in the new movie, he's the voice of Papa Smurf!)

New Smurfs T-shirts are now available at The Gap, and will be available through the release of the movie. Also there will be more Smurfs toys available than Gargamel can shake a stick at. A full line of toys from Jakks Pacific—including poseable Smurfs figures!

We're sure everyone must've enjoyed the giant Smurf balloon in the 2010 Macy's Thanksgiving Day Parade, not to mention the exclusive Holiday Smurf doll available exclusively from the famed department store.

Then came the surprise hit of the digital world—"The Smurfs' Village" free game app for the iPad, the iPod touch, and iPhone from Capcom Mobile. It's the highest-grossing app on the Apple Store due to players buying up so many Smurfberries as they build a virtual Smurfs' Village.

And all of the above is just the start. Smurfs-mania will kick in to high gear the sooner we get to the release of the Smurfs movie. Expect Smurfs toys at McDonald's, a Smurfs video game from Ubisoft for Nintendo Wii and Nintendo DS. Smurf toy prizes in popular kids' cereals from Kellogg's. With even more to come.

But obviously, what we're most excited about is seeing the original Smurfs comics by Peyo at long last back in print in North America. The comics are where it all started. When the Smurfs first appeared in "The Smurfs and the Magic Flute," a Johan and Peewit adventure, they instantly won the hearts of fans, and after a few more guest-appearances with Johan and Peewit, were awarded their own series, starting with "The Purple Smurfs." Many more comics followed, and the rest is history.

Speaking of that history, may we direct your attention to a new book written by our very own Smurfs Consultant, and writer of the Smurfology Blog, Matt Mu   s called "The World of Smurfs," a celeb   of tiny blue proportions. It hits bookstore shelves May 2011. "The World of Smurfs" traces Smurf history from their beginnings in Belgian magazine SPIROU to their popular Hanna-Barbera cartoon series to their upcoming feature film. Topics include: character bios (Papa Smurf, The Smurfette, Hefty, Gargamel, Azrael, and the rest); a brief intro to the Smurfs' creator, the artist Peyo; Smurf pop-cultural and live-action variations; and more! This timely tome is only $29.95, and may just be the most Smurf-tastic book ever.

No matter how you look at it, 2011 is shaping up as the Year of The Smurfs. And that's just smurfy!

Jim

YOU CAN'T SMURF IN THE WAY OF PROGRESS

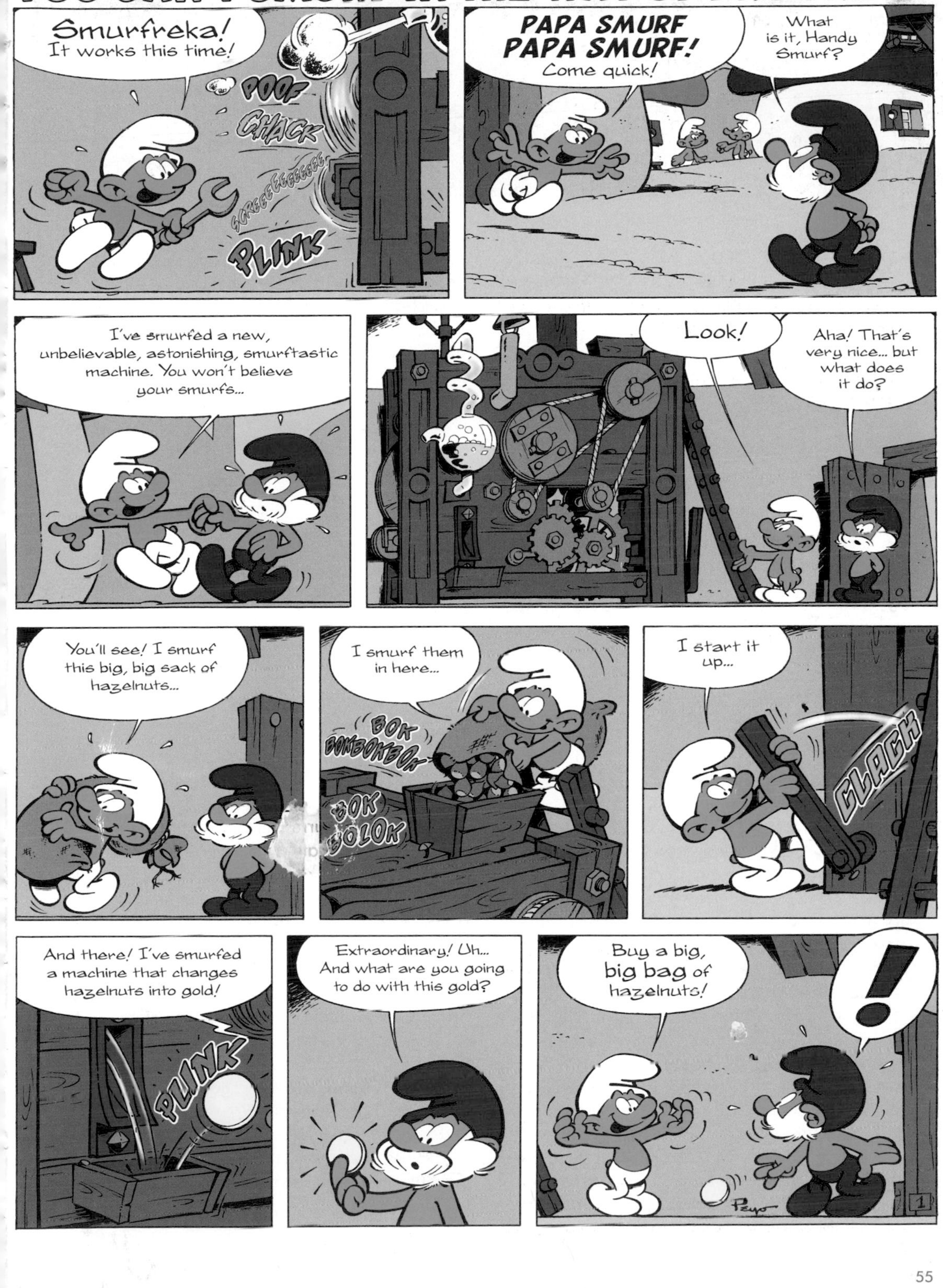

Smurfreka! It works this time!
POOF
CHACK
PLINK
PAPA SMURF PAPA SMURF! Come quick!
What is it, Handy Smurf?
I've smurfed a new, unbelievable, astonishing, smurftastic machine. You won't believe your smurfs...
Look!
Aha! That's very nice... but what does it do?
You'll see! I smurf this big, big sack of hazelnuts...
I smurf them in here...
BOK
BOKBOKBOK
BOK
BOLOK
I start it up...
CLACK
And there! I've smurfed a machine that changes hazelnuts into gold!
PLINK
Extraordinary! Uh... And what are you going to do with this gold?
Buy a big, big bag of hazelnuts!
!

SMURFS BIOS:
Gos (Roland Goosens)

Sharp-eyed Smurfs-fans will have noticed that in addition to Peyo's name on the cover, there's another signature as well—"Gos." Well, we checked online at www.lambiek.net, a truly valuable resource, and here's what we found...

Roland Goossens, better known as Gos, born January 3, 1937, was one of the popular artists that published in *SPIROU* magazine in the 1970s. Before turning to comics, Goossens worked in the Navy for eleven years. He devoted his spare time to comic strips, and his first story was published in the military magazine *NOS FORCES*. His professional comics career began when he joined Studio Peyo. There, he assisted Peyo on several episodes of "Les Schtroumpfs," as the Smurfs are called in French, and "Benoît Brisefer." At the same time, he created several short stories for the magazine. He also wrote scenarios for François Walthéry, including episodes of "Jacky et Célestin" and the first two adventures of "Natacha."

Gos had his breakthrough in 1969, when he took over the artwork of the popular "Gil Jourdan" series from Maurice Tillieux. He illustrated the series until Tillieux's death in 1979. In 1972, he also began a series of his own: "Khéna et le Scrameustache." This humorous and friendly science-fiction comic, about an extraterrestrial cat and his earth friend, became one of *SPIROU*'s most popular series. With adding such alien creatures as "Les Galaxiens" to the series, Gos developed an entire universe around his two main characters. Since the mid-1980s, Gos's son Walt assisted his father on the series, and later on began drawing gags with "Les Galaxiens" on his own.

(Special thanks to Bas at Lambiek Studio, for finding the photo of Gos. It's Gos in Studio Peyo in 1964, from the archives of Nine Culliford.)